DIARY OF A NERD

VOLUME 1

ABLAZE

to my Big Mind Kill
Philip Osbourne

A special thanks to my friend and my mentor
Brian Yuzna

PHILIP OSBOURNE
DIARY OF A NERD

The story of a very special kid who believes in fantasy (a lot!)

WRITTEN BY
Philip Osbourne

ILLUSTRATIONS BY
Roberta Procacci

ABLAZE

ABOUT THE AUTHOR

Philip Osbourne is a writer from Portsmouth, NH. In addition to writing Diary of a Nerd, he has worked on movie screenplays, comics projects and is the author of "Harry & Bunnie" and "ABC Monster", two cartoons produced by Animasia, among other works. The bestselling author is now published in 40 countries, and the success of his books will continue on in TV and movies.

FOR ABLAZE

MANAGING EDITOR
Rich Young
DESIGNER
Rodolfo Muraguchi

Publisher's Cataloging-in-Publication Data

Names: Osbourne, Philip, author.
Title: Diary of a Nerd: the story of a special boy who believes in fantasy (a lot) /
written and illustrated by Philip Osbourne.
Description: Portland, OR: Ablaze Publishing, 2020. | Summary: Phil, twelve, is a self-professed nerd...
an intellectual who enjoys spending his days with his friends, "The Geek Team".
Identifiers: ISBN: 978-1-950912-18-6
Subjects: LCSH Friendship—Juvenile fiction. | Diaries—Juvenile fiction. | Middle schools—
Juvenile fiction. | Schools—Juvenile fiction. | Humorous stories. | Graphic novels. |
Comic books, strips, etc. | CYAC: Friendship—Fiction. | Middle schools—Fiction. Schools—
Fiction. | Diaries—Fiction. | BISAC JUVENILE FICTION / Comics & Graphic Novels / General
Classification: LCC PZ7.7 .O766 2020 | DDC 741.5/973—dc23

BEFORE WE START
A proud young nerd
by Phil DICKENS a.K.a. PHIL THE NERD

I knew I was a nerd the day I turned 12. The present I asked my parents for my birthday was a LEGO REPRODUCTION of the **STAR WARS DEATH STAR**. It looks like a small moon with a huge laser cannon that could destroy a planet with one shot.

If you know **STAR WARS** you'll

understand why I

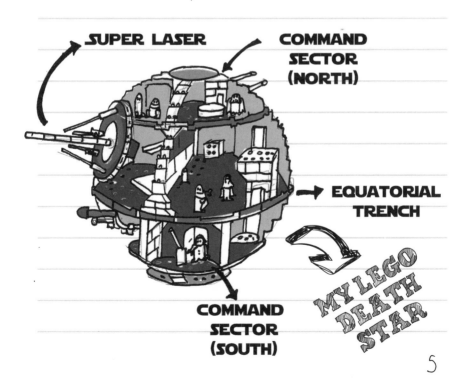

SUPER LASER

COMMAND SECTOR (NORTH)

EQUATORIAL TRENCH

COMMAND SECTOR (SOUTH)

MY LEGO DEATH STAR

love that toy so

much. If you don't, have a

quick look at the **Nerd**

Guides I've attached

throughout my Diary and

everything will be clearer. My birthday gift

from my friends was a **Daredevil** t-shirt. I was

so happy I almost cried tears of joy because **I**

love sci-fi movies and **SUPERHEROES!**

Later on, my friends and I watched

THE BIG BANG THEORY and had a great time

following Sheldon, Penny and all the other

characters' adventures. That's definitely my

favorite TV series. I like it because it's about

a group of really unusual

guys who are friends and love sharing their

hobbies and interests.

Frankly, It's about

nerds, just like

me.

My Daredevil t-shirt! I love it!

I could have thrown a different party for my 12th **BIRTHDAY**, but that's me, I'm a **NERD**.

I love using my imagination and I think it's **cool** to read physics books and comics and watch the weirdest tv shows. **That's why sometimes people make fun of me.**

I do all those amazing things commonly referred to as "**CRAZY NERD STUFF**".

I've been given a ton of nicknames: Trivial Man, WEEPING WONK, Bookworm, **BABY HAWKING**, **CHICKEN GEEK**. But after a while I became known as, simply, **PHIL THE NERD**! I wanted to know more about the definition of **NERD** and I found out that "**GEEK**" and "**NERD**" are two WORDS defining someone keen on new technologies, videogames, the internet, smartphones, etc.

But a nerd is more than that.

You should know that in the 90's "**NERD**" positively described someone

BILL GATES
The nerd who changed Information Technology

who **WAS GOOD WITH TECHNOLOGY.**

Bill Gates himself has often been called a **NERD**, but if it wasn't for him we'd still probably be using calculators and not Pcs. He invented WINDOWS, after all!

The creator of LINUX, **Linus Torvalds**, wrote in his autobiography that he was a nerd, too.

MIT **Professor Gerald Sussman** encouraged guys like me to be **PROUD** of ourselves when he said:

"My idea is to **PRESENT AN IMAGE TO CHILDREN** that it is good to be INTELLECTUAL, and not to care about the peer pressures to be ANTI-INTELLECTUAL. I want every child to turn into a NERD – where that means someone who prefers STUDYING AND LEARNING to competing for social dominance, which can unfortunately cause the downward spiral into social rejection."

Yes, we are weird! I won't deny it. Think about DILBERT, he was the hero of a super funny comic strip created by **Scott Adams**. When we talk about non-intellectual stuff sometimes we get totally lost, just like him.

Simpsons nerd

Jeff Albertson is not the usual "good" nerd. He's a know-it-all, quick-tempered and rude guy... not exactly a nice guy.

My draft

COMIC BOOK GUY!

nerd doc!

DILBERT PARODY

OUT! OUT! YOU DEMONS OF STUPIDITY!

DILBERT

DILBERT IS A COMIC STRIP BY SCOTT ADAMS

9

We're not super **COOL** people, nor are we all funny and nice. The Simpsons' Comic Book Guy, for instance, is really into comics and sci-fi

Velma Dinkley

NERDS OF THE PAST

Velma is the most clever member of Scooby Doo, she's the one with the brain who solves all investigations.

tv series like Star Trek and **STAR WARS** and he's definitely a cranky guy. NERDS WERE BORN A LONG TIME ago! Ask your parents what they'd call **VELMA DINKLEY** from **Scooby Doo**. She was a nerd! There's something you should know about NERDS, when a **NERD** gets the role of the hero in a story, they will probably have a secret identity as a superhero.

AM I THE REAL VELMA OR NOT?

Peter Parker a.k.a. Spider-man

PETER THE NERD

is a Science teacher and used to be the school's nerd. Clark Kent is **SUPERMAN's** alter ego and he's definitely a nerd. **CHUCK BARTOWSKI** from the tv series CHUCK is a new kind of a nerd. What I'm trying to say is that tv, movies and comics are packed with people JUST LIKE ME AND YOU! Am I filling your head with names you don't know? I told you already: **READ THE NERD GUIDES IN THE DIARY!** They'll give you insights into the NERDS' WORLD. If you're like me and people make fun of you, just laugh about it. Don't make the same mistakes I did. As you'll learn from the following pages, **it isn't worth it to hide or pretend** to be someone you're not.

The cartoon **FREAKAZOID'S** writers talked about **NERDS** in the episode titled 'NERDATOR': "...what they lack in physical prowess they make up in **brains**. Tell me, who writes all the **best selling books**? NERDS.

Chuck Bartowski
CHUCK

Chuck is a nerd. He's a good, down to earth guy. One day, he realized some of the US government's most important secrets had been uploaded to his brain.

Who makes all the **top grossing movies?** NERDS. Who designs **computer programs so complex** that ONLY THEY CAN USE THEM? NERDS. And who is running for **high public office?** No one **BUT NERDS.**"

So, heads up, my friends, be proud!

I am Phil, but you can call me **PHIL THE NERD.**

And I'm proud of it!

**READY?
IT'S TIME TO READ MY DIARY!
A NERD'S DIARY...**

BEFORE JOEY

Dear *Diary*,

Before I tell about what Joey said to me, **I WANT TO TELL YOU** a bit about him. He's got a strange perception of time, in fact he **USUALLY GETS TO SCHOOL LATE** but **GOES TO CONCERTS 8 HOURS BEFORE THEY BEGIN.**

Every time he's not prepared for school he brings up the **"DEATH IN THE FAMILY"** excuse. **HIS GRANDMOTHER MUST HAVE DIED AND RESURRECTED AT LEAST 9 TIMES.**

One day, he said to our teacher: "**I hate school. IT DRIVES ME CRAZY.**

I finally learn something - and then here comes the next chapter!"

That's when I realized the way his brain was organized:

5% names

3% telephone contacts

2% school stuff

90% **Facebook** posts

My PANTS ARE ON FIRE!

Who in the world doesn't peek at their friends' posts or pics on social networks?

October 10th

Joey's a SOCIAL VICTIM. Just to be clear, he can't help but connecting to social media every 3 minutes. Today, when leaving school, he was bragging: "Phil, I've reached 500 friends on **Facebook!**"

Some time ago my Dad told me: "You know, I haven't had one hundred friends in 42 years. How many friends can a human being really have? According to Dunbar it's 150. Not one more. He was a scientist and said this is the highest number of people we can keep in our emotional landscape."

15

I think my Dad was right so I said that to Joey and want to know what he did? He freaked out and treated me like an idiot.

"**YOU'RE DEFINITELY A TRUE NERD FROM ANOTHER WORLD!**" he said.

Well, ok. Maybe I exaggerated a bit with the whole **DUNBAR**'s "exact number" story but I really **THINK ONE CANNOT HAVE BILLIONS OF TRUE FRIENDS.**

I've never thought my **Facebook** friends had to be real friends.

Dear Diary, before I tell you what I think about it, I'd better explain how **CLASH OF CLANS** works.

The purpose of the game is to build a village and reach the highest number of trophies. The highest level consists of reaching the top of the national or worldwide chart by attacking other players' villages with your own army, storing resources in your own Country and building weapons for protection.

CLASH OF CLANS

Clash of Cans is a videogame developed by Supercell for iOS and Android and was first released on August 2nd 2012.

Players unite into CLANS, which are kind of like user groups.

Well, **friendship is a sort** of Clash of Clans, where you talk and collaborate.

If life was like Clash, my team would be made up of **4 people** and a **DOG,** and my **FRIENDS** and I would be a younger version of **The Big Bang Theory.**

Cool game!

WILD BEARDED BARBARIANS, WIZARDS, PYROMANIACS... THE UNSTOPPABLE ARMY OF CLASH OF CLANS.

In the series they're all university graduates living in Pasadena: **LEONARD HOFSTADTER**, experimental physicist, **SHELDON COOPER**, theoretical physicist, **HOWALRD WOLOWITZ**, rocket scientist and **RAJ KOOTHRAPPALI**, astrophysicist. They're FOUR YOUNG SCIENTISTS working together at the *CALIFORNIA INSTITUTE OF TECHNOLOGY*. They're all clever and "different." Real geeks and nerds, just like us.

RAJ
Doesn't talk to girls.

I'm telling you this because **SHELDON** and his friends spend their free time exactly **LIKE WE DO**: reading comics, playing video games, role-playing games and **WATCHING SCI-FI MOVIES AND TV SERIES.**

OK, GOT IT! You're getting bored and want me to introduce **my group of friends.** You're right!

SHELDON
theoretical physicist

LEGEND!
THE BIG BANG THEORY

DO YOU LIKE MY DRAWING?

GENIUS

THE BEST

SUPER

NERD 100%

Ok, my group! There are FOUR of us, plus a **dog**. WE'RE ALL A BIT WEIRD, BUT WHO ISN'T, after all? So, I'll start with my sister **Ellen**, an 8 year old with the *finest business acumen.*

Yes, she fantasizes about having her own fashion company. Do you find it normal to read finance newspapers at 8? She's scary. **Trust me!**

Determined!

ELLEN DICKENS

PHIL. AS SOON AS I START MY OWN COMPANY, I WANT YOU AS MY ASSISTANT.

8 yrs. old

THE NEW KINDLE FIRE OPERATING SYSTEM IS BUGGED. DON'T TELL ME YOU DIDN'T KNOW THAT?

She's just a kid, but she speaks like a super ambitious ECONOMICS GRADUATE!

She plans everything in detail, not like me.

She's determined and loves being our leader.

She's the youngest but IT DOESN'T STOP HER FROM MAKING DECISIONS FOR ALL OF US. Don't ask me how she does it, but she **MANAGES TO PLAN** our days from top to bottom. One more thing she loves is yelling at us: "HURRY UP! IT's ALMOST TOMORROW!"

She must always optimize and save time!

As if she had a crazy schedule at 8 yrs. old.

CRAZY!

Member #2 is **George**, a.k.a.
"**YOUNGTWEETY**." He's 14, 2 years older than
me, and his dream is to become the new
Zuckerberg.

Mark Elliot Zuckerberg is an American computer scientist and entrepreneur. He's one of the five creators of Facebook and the owner of Instagram.

WONDERING about his nickname? Easy!
George doesn't speak very much. He's got a
140-character limit. Yes, you got it, he always
speaks as if he's tweeting something. He'd use
EMOTICONS  to express himself when
speaking, if that was possible. He's the perfect
student. The best in science, but the worst at
sports. He's a bit clumsy. He's very funny, he
reminds me of Chewbacca from **STAR WARS.**

My Georgebacca is terrible! You can watch him on George Wars!

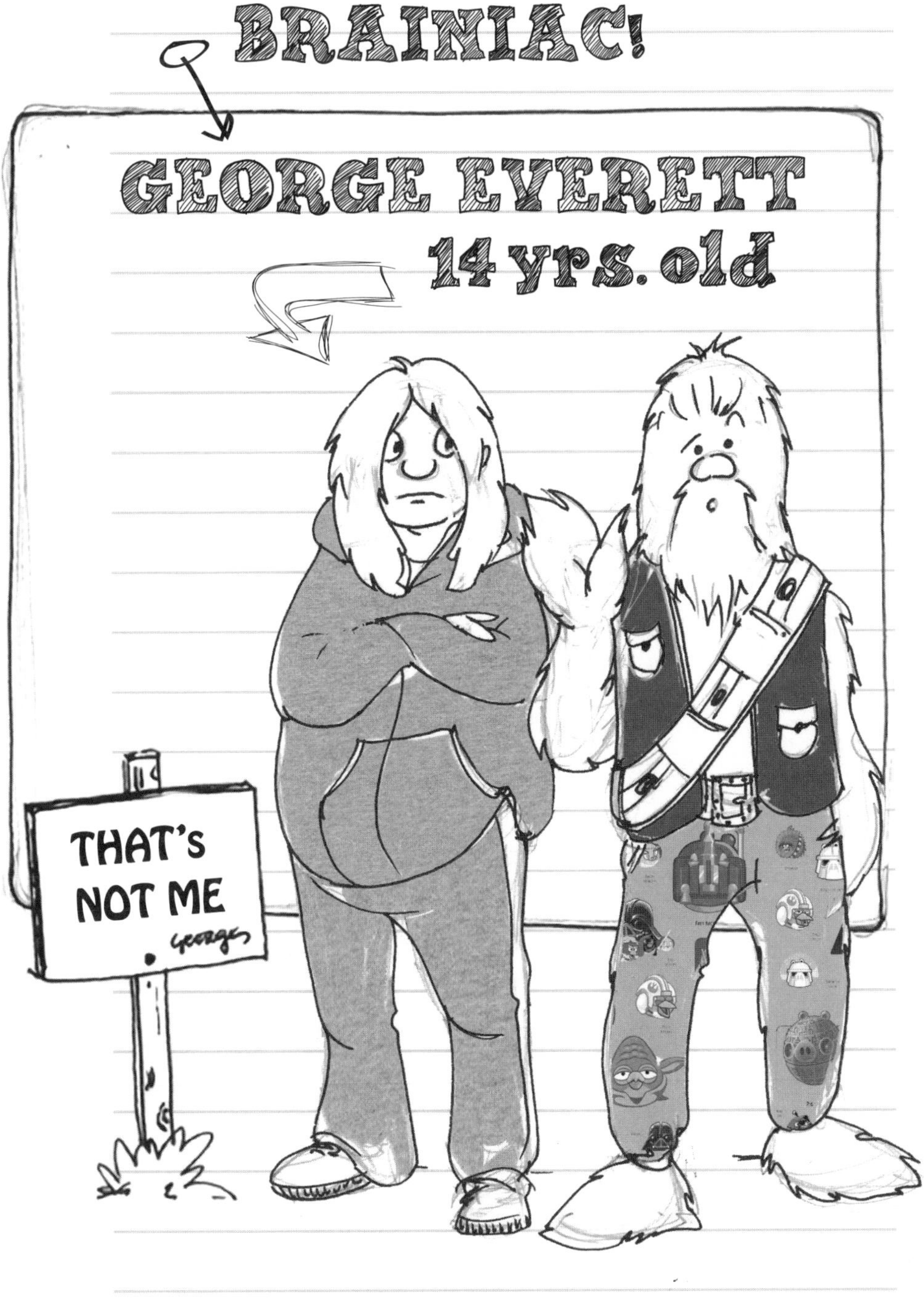
BRAINIAC!
GEORGE EVERETT
14 yrs. old
THAT's NOT ME
george

GEORGE

George's parents are obsessed with symmetry. they are engineers that are always lining him up with everything in the house.

Next is **Nicholas**. He's my own age, loves watching FOOTBALL on TV and keeps on **GOOGLING** Miss "Dance" Ann on his tablet. She's a girl he's deeply in love with. She will never know how he feels **BECAUSE HE'S REALLY SHY.** I mean, really. When he sees a girl, he runs away as fast as he can, doesn't even want to be recognized. That's why he always wears **A PAPER BAG ON HIS HEAD.** I suppose he doesn't want to show how embarassed he feels. You know what's funny about him? **His INSANE ideas.** NICHOLAS is very clever, though he doesn't always put his **TALENTS TO THE BEST USE.**

For example, he invented this **LIGHTNING-RESISTANT TABLET.**

Now why in the world would anyone need to use an Ipad in a **THUNDERSTORM** (while risking electrocution?)

During our last summer vacation, he

SPENT A MONTH WORKING ON A PROJECT:

he came up with a scale that could weigh every single person going in and out of a shopping center. **Why?** It is as simple as this:

HE WANTED TO TRACK DOWN ROBBERS.

How? His scale weighed and registered all the people going in and out of the shopping center when they were at the cashier. If someone weighed more at the exit than when he or she entered and didn't stop at the cashier, the scale would sound an alarm.

It was a perfect invention!

It was a high-precision scale and each and everyone's features were saved on a computer.

DON'T YOU THINK THAT'S PURE GENIUS?

IT WAS ACTUALLY ABSURD!

Why? Because if someone had, for instance, held his wife's bag for a second or had eaten a pizza in the meantime, his weight would've increased and the scale would have set off the alarm. BASICALLY HIS INVENTION WAS AS FASCINATING as it was USELESS!

Nicholas had spent almost his entire vacation on something completely worthless!

That's so typical of Nicholas.

NICHOLAS LEE
12 Yrs. Old.
Shy!

Member 4 is not a human being: **MY DOG,**
Teo! Teo Messi, like the Barcelona
soccer player, because as soon as he sees a
ball, he goes crazy. Teo was my parents gift
to **ELLEN WHEN SHE LOST**
HER FIRST TOOTH.

My dog is not like the Griffins' Brian — he
doesn't talk or drive, and he is **VERY NICE WITH**
ME AND MY FRIENDS.

Not so much with strangers though.
He **WOULD BE** a normal
dog, if it wasn't for his attitude.
He's got more human in
him than dog. In fact,
he does what we do..

BRIAN is one of the protagonists of Family Guy, a
cartoon series created by Seth MacFarlane.

Brian

But especially the things we shouldn't. My
parents are **not part of the team**
but **THEY ARE A PART OF**
MY LIFE and I'm going to tell you a
little about them.

TEO MESSI OUR LITTLE DOG!

HUMANIZED.

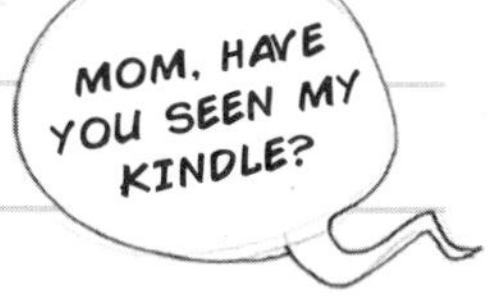
MOM, HAVE YOU SEEN MY KINDLE?

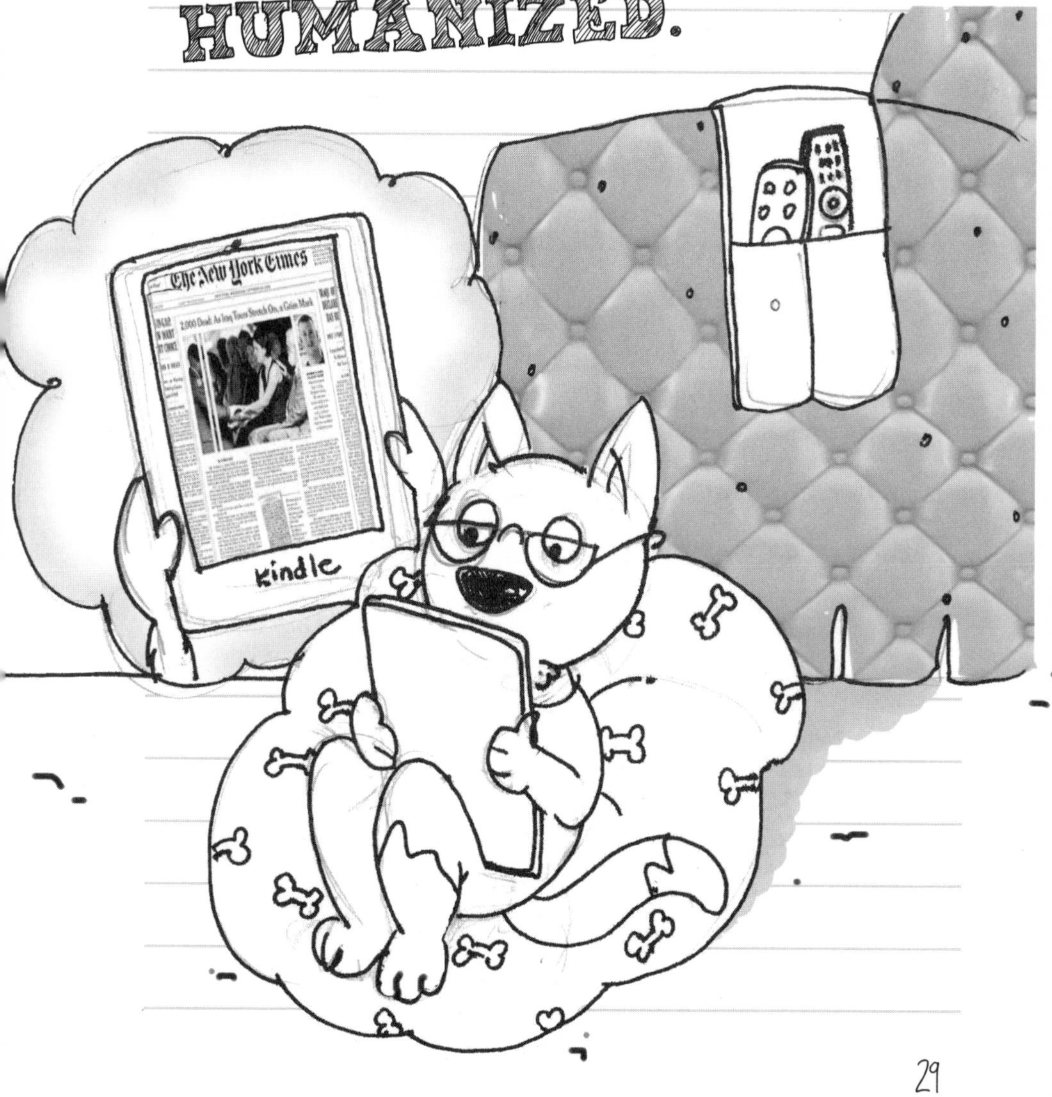
The New York Times
kindle

Lenny and **Marilyn** aren't quite like my friends' parents. Well, **THAT'S A LiE.** They are SO not like my friends' parents! Mom's **the only woman in the world** who wants her son to play sports without sweating. **I'll be running** on a sunny beach in August and she goes: "Just DON'T **SWEAT HONEY!**" Maybe I sweated too much when **I WAS A KID**?

If I stay in the bathroom for more than 3 minutes, she calls the **FIRE DEPARTMENT.** I'd say she's just a little overprotective. **MOM GOT FAMOUS** when she designed a successful line of dark, tongue-in-cheek t-shirts. Blogs and magazines say she's **REALLY COOL.** Her Instagram page reached **100,000 LIKES** and her t-shirt quotes are among the **MOST TWEETED HASHTAGS.** Her **SKETCHBOOKS, T-SHIRTS** and **MY FAMILY'S PICS** are on Pinterest. She's always thinking about creating new Tees.

CRAAAAAAAAAZY!

MOM'S MOST COMMON QUOTE:

DON'T SWEAT!

TWO OF MOM'S T-SHIRTS -
I'LL BE GOOD IF YOU'LL BE GOOD!

I'LL BE GOOD IF YOU'LL BE GOOD!

I must confess, I don't quite understand my mom's t-shirts' success, but people find them funny.

Dad was a LICENSING MANAGER for a company producing card games until he JUST DIDN'T FEEL LIKE SELLING RIGHTS ANYMORE.

He was fed up with WORKING AS A MANAGER, so he quit and got himself a studio far away from the city where he writes stories and essays about UFOS.
His LATEST BOOK is sold on Amazon and I suppose people love reading about his research and ideas. He's no ordinary dad. HE'S GOT A WEIRD SENSE OF HUMOR. You never really understand whether he's joking or BEING SERIOUS. I remember hearing him once talking calmly to an old friend of his, saying: "Aliens are here. They're looking for clever, classy and charming life forms. HURRY, RUN. HIDE!" Everybody looked at my dad in shock for a moment – then they burst out laughing when THEY REALIZED HE MADE A JOKE.

Just to tell you a **LITTLE BIT MORE ABOUT DAD,** here's another story for you. He was taking me to **SCHOOL** and parking his car when **I ASKED HIM IF HE REALLY BELIEVED ALIENS EXISTED.**

Here is what he answered:

"UFOs DO exist. The Air Force does NOT". Here's another joke of his:

"WHAT DO UFOS DRINK?"

"I DON'T KNOW, DAD!"

Here came the punchline:

"TEA: AND NO FLYING SAUCER, PLEASE." HE'S ONE OF A KIND.

One more: **"PHIL, WHAT IS AN ALIEN's FAVORITE PLACE ON A COMPUTER?"**

I was speechless.

"The Space bar!"

Dad shouted.

LENNY A

DAD! A MISFIT!

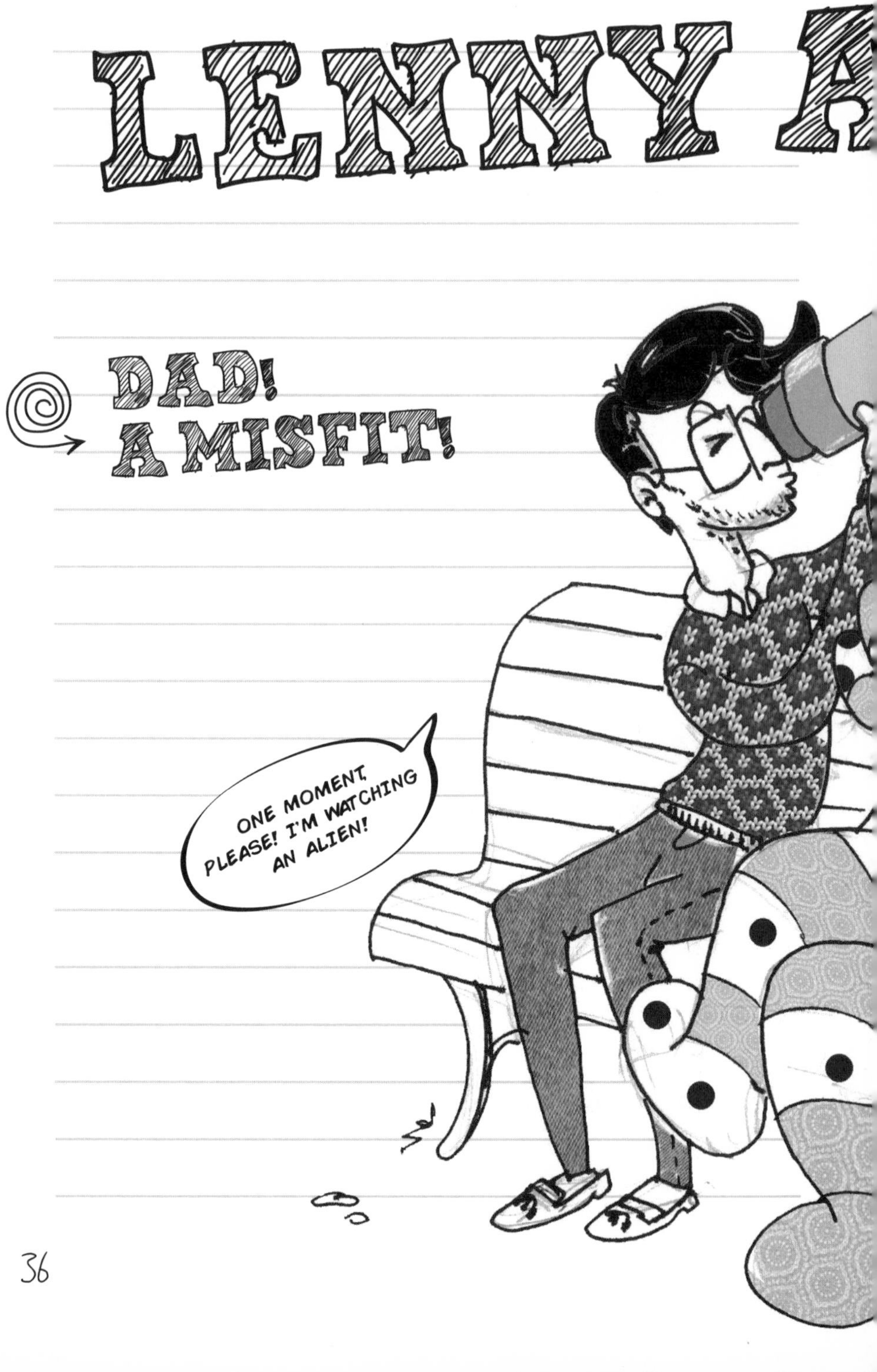
ONE MOMENT, PLEASE! I'M WATCHING AN ALIEN!

ND UFOS!

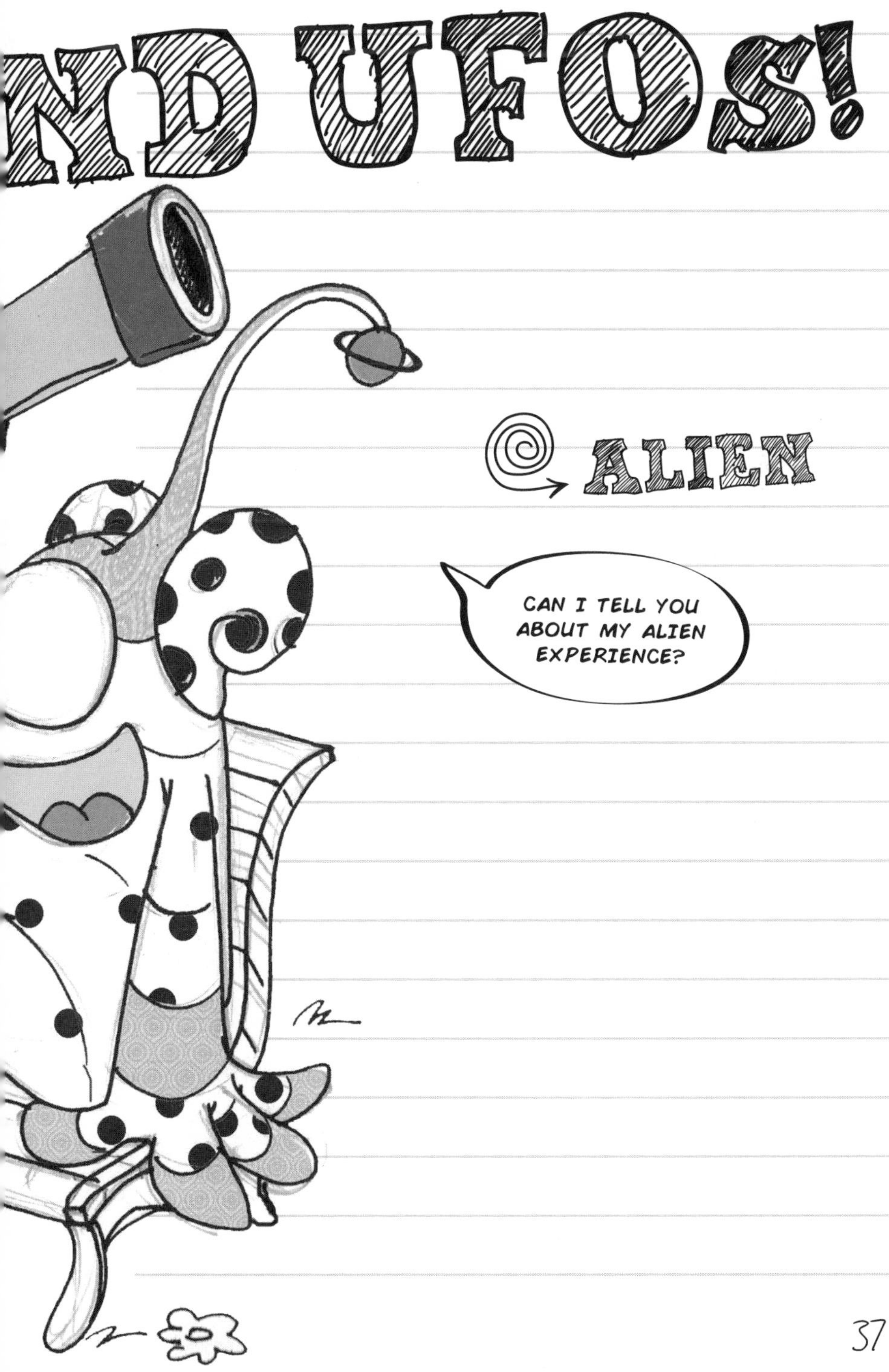
ALIEN
CAN I TELL YOU ABOUT MY ALIEN EXPERIENCE?

I'm Phil Dickens.

Not Philip K. Dick, the famous author who wrote **Blade Runner.**

Philip Kindred Dick was an American writer. When he was alive he was only famous in the sci-fi world, but later he became much more appreciated by both critics and a wider audience.

PHIL OSBOURNE

PHIL DICK
Writer

I'm from **Manhattan.** Yes, I'm one of the 8 million people living in the **NYC** commercial area. I live in Midtown, which is quite close to ROCKEFELLER CENTER, BROADWAY and TIMES SQUARE. From my house, I can see the most famous and the tallest buildings, the EMPIRE STATE BUILDING and 432 PARK AVENUE.

I love math, physics, the Rubik's cube (I can solve it

in 16 seconds) and my dream
is to become like **Albert Einstein**
one day. I also wish I'd had the
chance to meet **Stephen Hawking**
and talk to him.

ALL THE FACTS I JUST LISTED REALLY DON'T HELP ME GET ALONG WELL WITH BULLIES AT SCHOOL. Two weeks ago,
I wanted to make friends with a guy so
I asked him: "**WHAT DO YOU KNOW ABOUT ARCHIMEDES' ARGUMENTS?**"

I was hoping to start a conversation but he
replied: "Well, bro, I didn't have anything to
do with the whole thing! He started it!"

You must have things clear by now: studying to me
doesn't mean getting distracted by texting,
eating, surfing online and watching tv while
reading a book. And I love numbers.
I enjoy studying them and interpreting them.
For instance:

I was born on 05/23

23 is made up of 2 and 3. 2+3 = 5 and that's the month I was born. Every number of my date of birth leads to 5.

You think I'm nuts? I'm not! I just love finding coincidences and interpreting them. **AND THIS IS WHY PEOPLE AT SCHOOL ARE ALWAYS MAKING FUN OF ME.** I've never been the school's clown. I've always been the trapeze artist because I'm always suspended! That's nothing to laugh about!

THIS IS THE REASON WHY I'VE DECIDED TO CHANGE.

Shhhhhh...

If I had met...
STEPHEN HAWKING

do you think my questions would have bothered him?

WHAT KIND OF CHANGE? I promise I'm gonna tell you. One thing you should know is that everything started with an **Albert Einstein** quote: "*LOGIC WILL GET YOU FROM A TO B. IMAGINATION WILL TAKE YOU EVERYWHERE*".

LAUREN

the most beautiful girl!

ALBERT EINSTEIN

The theory of relativity

My hero!

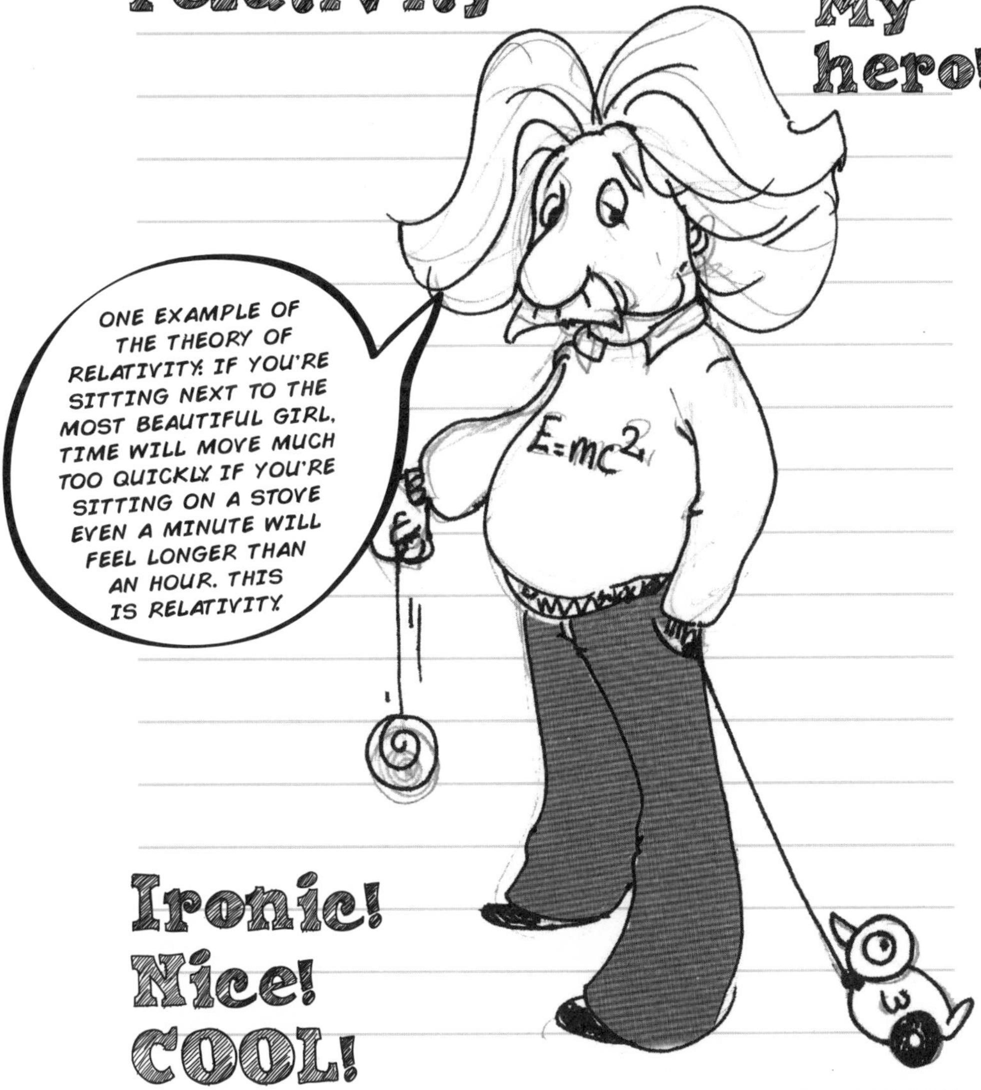
ONE EXAMPLE OF THE THEORY OF RELATIVITY: IF YOU'RE SITTING NEXT TO THE MOST BEAUTIFUL GIRL, TIME WILL MOVE MUCH TOO QUICKLY. IF YOU'RE SITTING ON A STOVE EVEN A MINUTE WILL FEEL LONGER THAN AN HOUR. THIS IS RELATIVITY.
$E=mc^2$

Ironic!
Nice!
COOL!

ME, LAUREN AND MY INEPTITUDE

I haven't got a girlfriend, but I think **LAUREN** IS AMAZING. We're in the same class. I love it when she wears her jean skirt and star-shaped earrings.

I'd love to have a pair of rocket-shaped glasses to get in her galaxy. I tried to talk to her several times and one time I managed to do it! I told her that the **MICHELSON-MORLEY** experiment demonstrated that with reference to the speed of light, there is no displacement of the interference bands. I DON'T THINK SHE APPRECIATED my pick-up line. I wish I could be like an ANGRY BIRD and act without thinking twice, but I just can't... so I usually quit and go back to the numbers. Girls **PARALYZE** me!

Like
ANGRY BIRDS

I'd fall on Lauren and talk to her!

nerd bird

45

December 11th

Today, I went to the library and ran into **Lauren.** It was as if she was **WAITING FOR ME.** I wish I had told her I was going to the **COMIC SHOP** next, then to the same theater that I had seen her for the first time. I was only a few feet from her when **my heart started** pounding like a **drum** and I switched to the "I need to pee" mode. I couldn't say anything. **WHAT IF SHE TOLD ME I WAS A CRAZY LUNATIC AND A BRAINIAC MISFIT?** I couldn't speak a word, so I just ran away like **AN IDIOT.** Luckily I had **Teo** with me and he comforted me with a **COUPLE OF LICKS.**

How can I be such a massive chicken nerd?

SLURP!

46

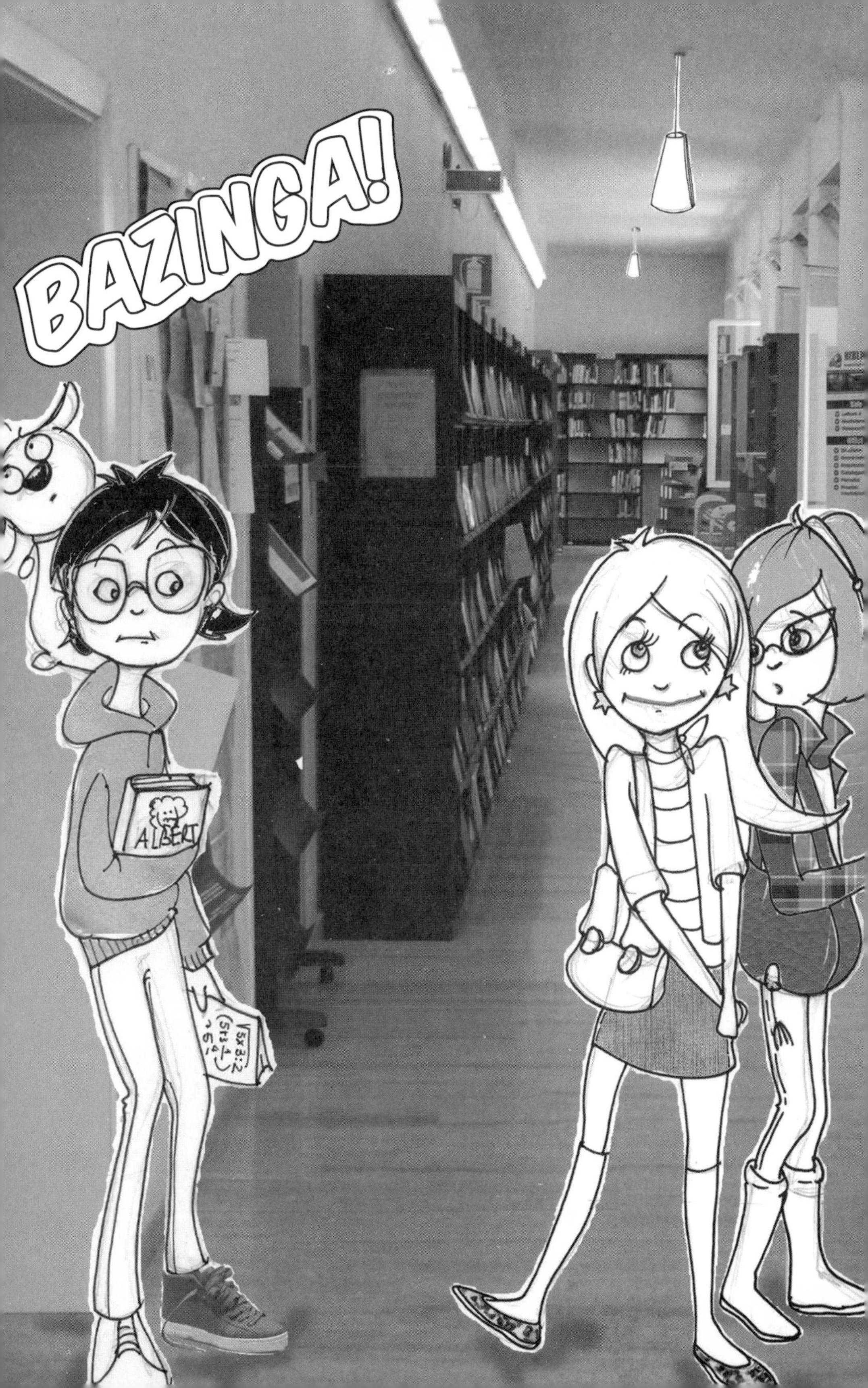
BAZINGA!
ALBERT

December 16th

Tonight, I had a dream about **DARTH VADER!**
He looked so real, it felt crazy!

Can't believe it was all just a dream:

he came up to my bed, speaking with his scary voice. "What do you want?" I asked him. "**I FIND YOUR LACK OF FAITH DISTURBING.**" he replied.

You can't be real!

"**IT'S ABOUT TIME YOU TAKE UP A LIGHTSABER AND LET THE WORLD KNOW THE REAL DARK SIDE OF THE FORCE,**" he ordered, angrily.
I was really scared. How could DARTH VADER, an imaginary character, possibly visit me in my dreams to show me the right way?

I got up from my bed and found an email alert on my Ipad.

It was a newsletter announcing new fencing courses to sign up for.

MY DREAM WITH DARTH VADER

THE STRANGE APPARITION

HOLD ON A SEC!!!!!!!!! LET'S STOP THE DIARY FOR A MINUTE!

DARTH VADER(?)

DO YOU KNOW WHO I AM?
I'M ANAKIN SKYWALKER AS IMAGINED BY PHIL. I'M ALSO
DARTH VADER IN STAR WARS AND IN SPITE OF WHAT GEORGE
LUCAS SAYS ABOUT ME I AM THE HERO OF THE WHOLE
FRANCHISE.

WAS IT A SIGN?

I don't know why, but I told my parents about the dream. Well, Mom makes money with little **MONSTERS** and Dad sees **ALIENS** all the time, so convincing them to let me take **fencing** classes was far from difficult. I didn't say anything to my friends. **THEY SEE ME AS PHIL THE NERD**, the bookworm. Like **Peter Parker** aka **Spider-man**. They'd never see me as **THE SPORTY TYPE**. Just **the contrary!** They probably think of me more like an old **Pac-man**, running through labyrinths and **EATING STRAWBERRIES**.

JUST A SECOND, BEFORE WE PICK UP WHERE I LEFT OFF...

PAC-MAN

It was my dad who first introduced me to Pac-man. It's a famous videogame created by Toru Iwatani for Midway Games in 1980 as an arcade game. Many different versions for almost every console and pc were created afterwards, turning it into the most famous videogame ever. The player controls Pac-Man through a maze while eating pac-dots. Four enemies are trying to catch Pac-Man through the maze, if one of them touches him, he loses one of his lives. It's so COOL!

December 18th

Today, we stayed at my house.
George was **ENTHUSIASTIC**, but I couldn't
quite figure out why. He kept on repeating
we have to give ourselves a name for the
MATH & **SCIENCE COMPETITION**: "THE
NERD TRIO." He said **Nicholas** and
I had to beat all the school seniors! But I
knew it wouldn't be that easy!
"YOU'RE GOING TO BEAT THEM! YOU'RE THE
BEST! TOGETHER WE'RE AS GOOD AS THE GUYS
FROM LAST YEAR. LET'S GET TRAINING AND
TAKE THEM BY SURPRISE! THEY WON'T SEE
US COMING! WE'RE NOTHING BUT KIDS TO
THEM," George said. Nicholas added: "I've
also made our costumes for the competition,
Star Trek-style.
"Who paid for them?"
I asked.

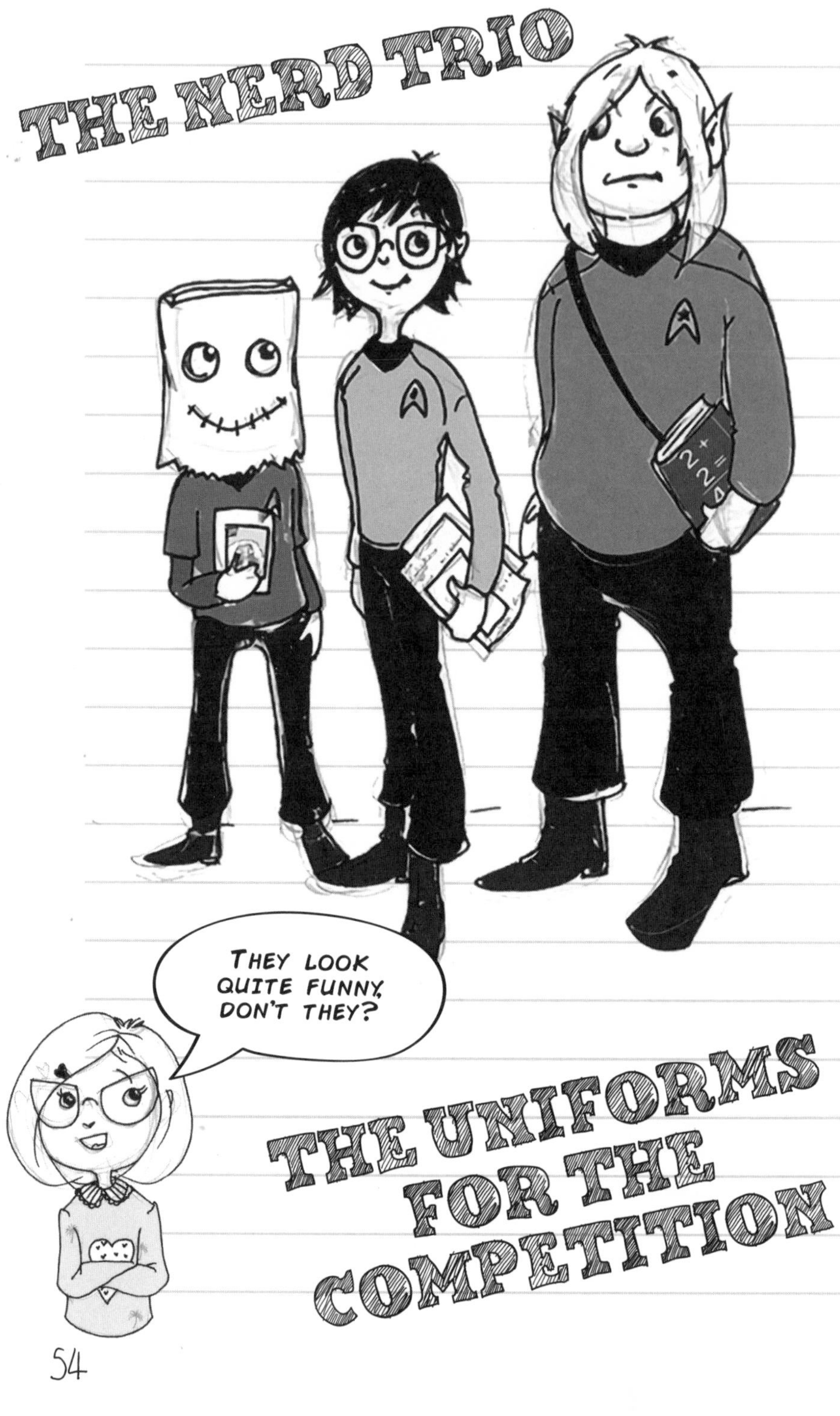
THE NERD TRIO
THEY LOOK QUITE FUNNY, DON'T THEY?
THE UNIFORMS FOR THE COMPETITION

I saw Ellen smirking while playing with Teo. **"CROWDFUNDING**, obviously", she answered. Her eyes twinkled.

"ONLINE BACKERS FINANCED OUR PROJECT AFTER CHECKING NICHOLAS' costume designs". What **WE HAVE TO DO NOW IS WIN THE FIRST PRIZE**, sell the Mac the winners will be given and pay our investors!"

"Your sister terrifies me!" said George, **"BUT SHE'S RIGHT!"** I didn't know what to say. I had to get ready to train for my first fencing tournament and didn't want Lauren to laugh at me while I was holding

The Mac to win!

the International Mega-Nerd Cup of the Year.

She would think I was nothing but a super geek and would never find me interesting. How on earth would a guy who just won a Math competition be attractive? But then I saw the look in my sister's and friends' eyes and I realized **I COULD DO ANYTHING I WANTED, IF BOTH REALITIES COULD BE JOINED TOGETHER.**

Dear *Diary*, you've just met my team, my real **friends**!

What my dad and Joey said made me think about myself a bit... I am nothing but a **NERD** to everyone at school but, hey, **THEY DON'T REALLY KNOW ME! MY REAL FRIENDS KNOW EVERYTHING ABOUT ME AND THEY STILL LIKE ME FOR WHO I AM!**

Ellen, Nicholas and George are **MY BEST FRIENDS** and I've got nothing to hide when I'm with them. **I CAN BE MYSELF BECAUSE THEY'RE HONEST AND TRUE TO ME.**

They're a part **OF MY LIFE** and I am a part of theirs. We spend our days together, we share **our dreams** and they don't think my hobbies are ridiculous or that I'm boring.

We share the same interests.

Maybe **DUNBAR** was wrong...maybe it IS possible to have more than **150 friends**, after all. If that turns to be true, **I WANT THEM TO BE LIKE MY TEAM!**

A team of nerds... but **REALLY**

SPECIAL
NERDS!

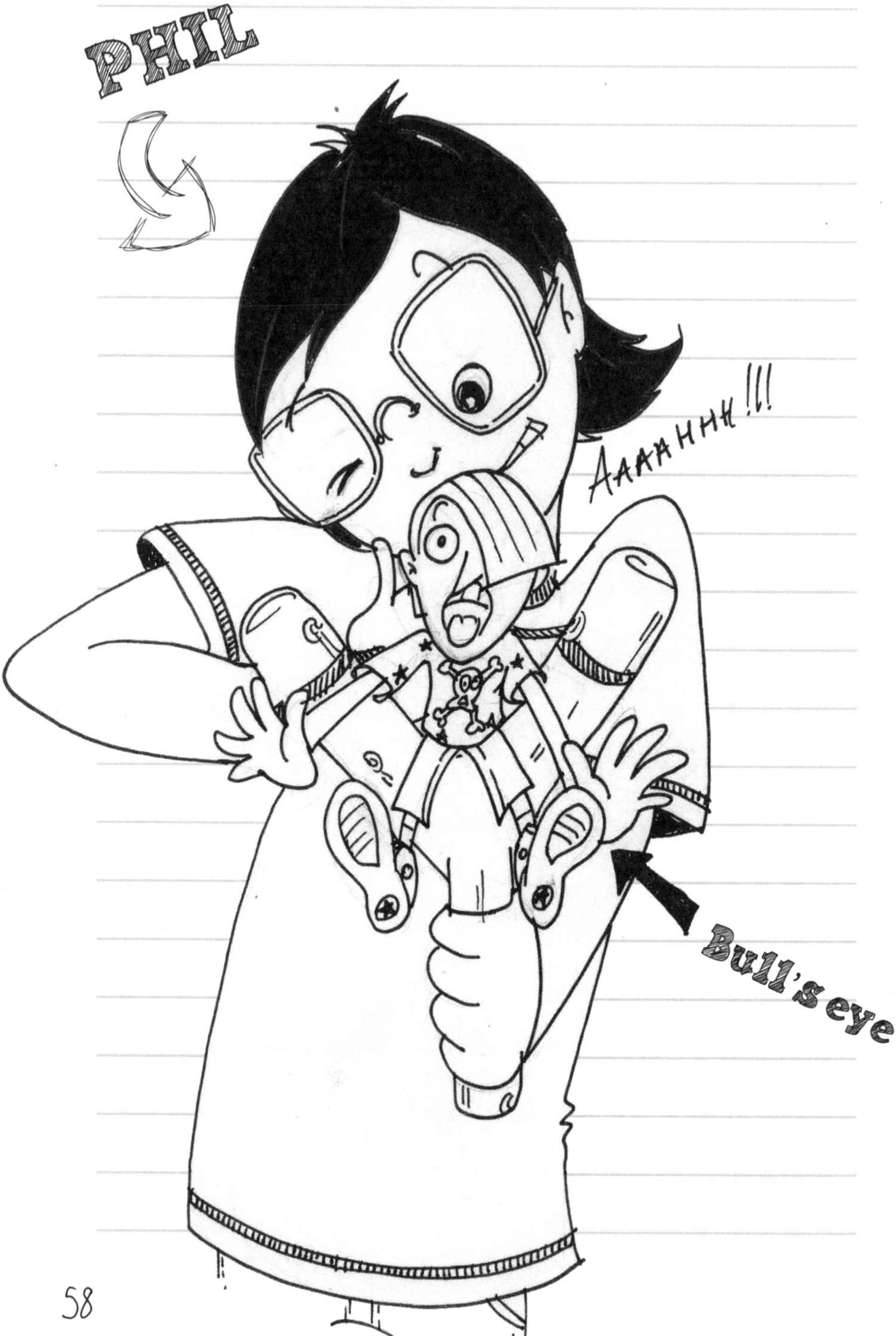
PHIL
AAAAHHH!!!
Bull's eye

Phil's note

A little break, stop reading! Since I've decided to

release my diary in full, you should know
that everything began on the days between
January 14th and 16th, so... read
carefully what I'm going
to tell you!

The day I met Lauren was the day I made up
my mind about doing something very stupid.
Since that very moment I've been telling
lies... MANY lies!

There's an old Russian saying: "With lies
you may go ahead in the world, but you
can never go back." If only I had known
that before... At the time, I was sure my
brain would've helped me out of any
risky situation, but I was wrong. I was
overestimating myself and I had no clue
about how complicated things would
become.

We often lie when we're scared of things we don't know, about what other people may think or what we may find out about ourselves... but the truth is, every time we lie, we get weaker, and our fears grow stronger.

It didn't take long to understand the mess I had put myself in with all those lies. Ghost Rider is a great movie. Now, that's a lie!

Ghost Rider is such a TERRIBLE movie!

December 21st

Today I had my **FIRST** fencing match! It was **A CITY COMPETITION**, with almost **250 competitors.** A lot of guys were much more prepared than me, **both technically and physically,** and I felt like **I had no chance at winning.** Before walking on the platform, I thought about all the things I had learned during **MY FIRST TWO MONTHS OF TRAINING:** I knew what a thrust, a lunge, a parry and a counter attack were. I was well aware of the fact I had chosen the épée as my fencing sword and the only thing I had to do was hit my opponent on any part of his body. I was really

SCARED, but the mask hid my face. I've always been Phil the Weak. **PHIL THE NERD.** What if things didn't turn out perfectly like it happens when I do math? It was always easy for me to deal with numbers...

Right before the match, I went to the bathroom for the tenth time and there I met **Darth Vader**, again.

"SO WE MEET AGAIN, KID!" he told me. "Am I hallucinating right now?" I thought. **"IT'S YOUR MOMENT NOW! OBI-WAN AND I ARE WAITING FOR YOU, THINGS HAVE COME FULL CIRCLE. WHEN I LEFT YOU I WAS BUT THE STUDENT, NOW I AM THE MASTER."** I thought he was just some lunatic quoting the movie lines.

"But I'm not Obi-Wan," I replied.

"YOU HAVE TO FIGHT!" he ordered.

"I'm not technically prepared, but I can try."

"DO. OR DO NOT. THERE IS NO TRY."

I thought about what Obi-Wan Kenobi would do and I said: "Only a Sith deals in absolutes. I'll do what I must."

I walked out of the bathroom and onto the platform.

STAR WARS IS ONLY A MOVIE? RIGHT?, MR DARTH VADER, ARE YOU REAL?

After 16 rounds, I was announced the winner. I don't know how it happened, but apparently I won! **NOW I'M PHIL, THE FENCING CHAMPION.**

Fencing is great and comes naturally to me.

I LOVE THE SPORT AND I LOVE THE TOURNAMENTS. But I didn't want the others **TO KNOW THAT THE NERD HAS TURNED INTO A WINNER.** I couldn't let them know about this... so before **I WENT ONSTAGE TO GET MY PRIZE, AN IDEA SUDDENLY CAME TO ME.** I saw a jacket left by a guy named **MIKE** on the platform and I put it on. His name was written in giant letters on both the front and the back of the jacket. I took my glasses off and had my picture taken. **SO, NOW I'VE GOT SOME PICTURES FOR MIKE THE FENCING CHAMPION.** I started a new **Instagram profile** and posted them there. **I lied** to everyone because I didn't want my nerd friends to think I'm a sporty guy and I didn't want all the sporty guys to know that everyone laughs at me because I'm a nerd. **Each and every nerd** in comics has a secret identity! **MIKE'S MINE NOW!**

After all... **NO ONE'S EVER FOUND OUT THAT CLARK KENT IS SUPERMAN!** ARE THEY ALL NUTS? YOU JUST HAVE TO TAKE OFF HIS GLASSES AND MESS WITH HIS HAIR A BIT! AND NO ONE HAS EVER RECOGNIZED HIM? HOW'S THAT POSSIBLE? IF I WORE A PAIR OF SUPERHERO TIGHTS EVEN TEO WOULD FIND OUT WHO I AM AND TELL ME I LOOK LIKE A LUNATIC!

Phil in tights is nothing but the usual **NERD**. But what about **PHIL WITH NO GLASSES**, wearing someone else's jacket, wet hair and a trophy in his hands? **WELL, THAT'S DIFFERENT**. Who would ever think that's me? **I LIVE WHERE BOOKS ARE, NOT IN THE GYM. That's not my natural habitat!** But it's different for Mike, my new cousin. **WELCOME TO MY LIFE, MIKE!** Welcome to my social media pages and, very soon, to Lauren's life. I know I can do it!

TEO IS A CHIHUAHUA

I SMELL PROBLEMS! PHIL AND MIKE ARE THE SAME PERSON! HOW'S HE GOING TO HANDLE IT? HE'LL MAKE A MESS. I KNOW THE TRUTH. WE GREAT DANES ARE NOT LIARS.

Hi, Do you know **Usain Bolt**? He's the person who ran **100 METERS IN LESS THAN 10 SECONDS!**

The great **Valentina Vezzali** is **DETERMINED AS WELL**, she won a lot of fencing competitions! I like people who fight and want to break records! They love challenges!

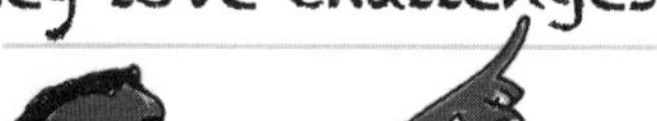
BOLT

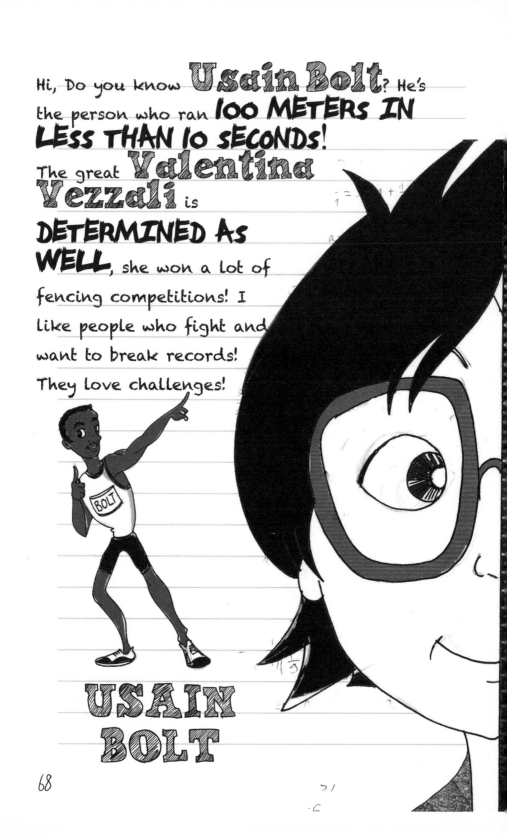

USAIN BOLT

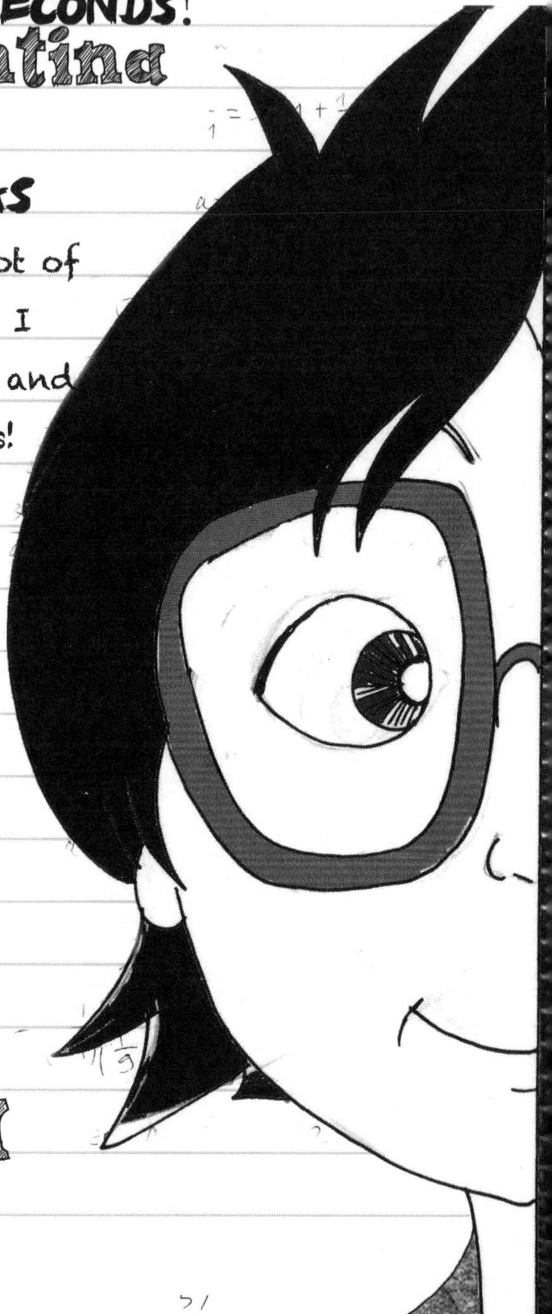

It's just a little lie, totally harmless.

I never thought sports could be so thrilling. **YOU HAVE TO BE REALLY DETERMINED** to get through all the matches and I never thought I was! Sure, participating is important, but if I had won second place I wouldn't have won silver... **I'd have lost gold, right?**

Anyway, I won **MY FIRST COMPETITION!**
I'll probably lose many others but that's definitely **A GOOD START!** Now **I JUST HAVE TO KEEP ON TRAINING AND BE READY FOR MY OPPONENTS.** Winning **the National Trophy** is my next goal.

HEART OR CUBE?

But first I want to win Lauren's **HEART**. As you probably figured out now, I had a **great idea**. What if it was **Mike** who wins Lauren's love? **SHE DOESN'T EVEN LOOK AT ME NOW BECAUSE I'M A NERD!** But a less intellectual fencing champion would certainly look appealing to her!

But the Science Competition is in two days and I'm already worried about what everyone will say: "**WHAT? WHO ARE YOU DATING NOW?**" They'll ALSO make fun of us because of our STAR TREK costumes. **I LOVE THE UNIFORMS AND I LOVE SCIENCE**, physics and math but **INSULTS** will **NOT** make me look **POPULAR OR COOL**, certainly not to Lauren. To win her, I'll have to **bring Mike** into her life.

I've got the perfect plan, and **SOCIAL MEDIA** will prove to be very useful... IT'LL **TAKE ME TWO CLICKS** to get a **NEW PROFILE**, two more to open a fake website with fake news about **MIKE** and two final clicks to "like" my **DEAR IMAGINARY** cousin's page and pics.

After sending Lauren a friend request, I'll ask her out. Sorry, not me, Mike will.

It's as simple as that! And at that point, I'll be able to **CUT THE ROPE** like in the videogame and finally approach her.

January 12th

I stayed in bedroom all day, **READING THROUGH AN OLD ISSUE** of **Spider-man**. It was a reprint of the first issue written by **STAN LEE** and drawn by **STEVE DITKO**. In that story, **PETER PARKER** was lying to everyone and things didn't end up going well for his uncle Ben...

I leafed through it and it felt as if I was looking at a mirror. I didn't know whether to tell my friends I was a fencing champion because my nerd friends wouldn't understand and the sporty guys wouldn't respect me either 'cause they'd see me as an intruder in their private world. Are you wondering why I haven't come forward to Lauren myself? I want to win her over, but... she'd never bother even looking at a nerd. She dated Ted for months. He's the captain of the football team and actually looks more like a wrestler than a nerd. Lauren talks to the athletes not to nerds.

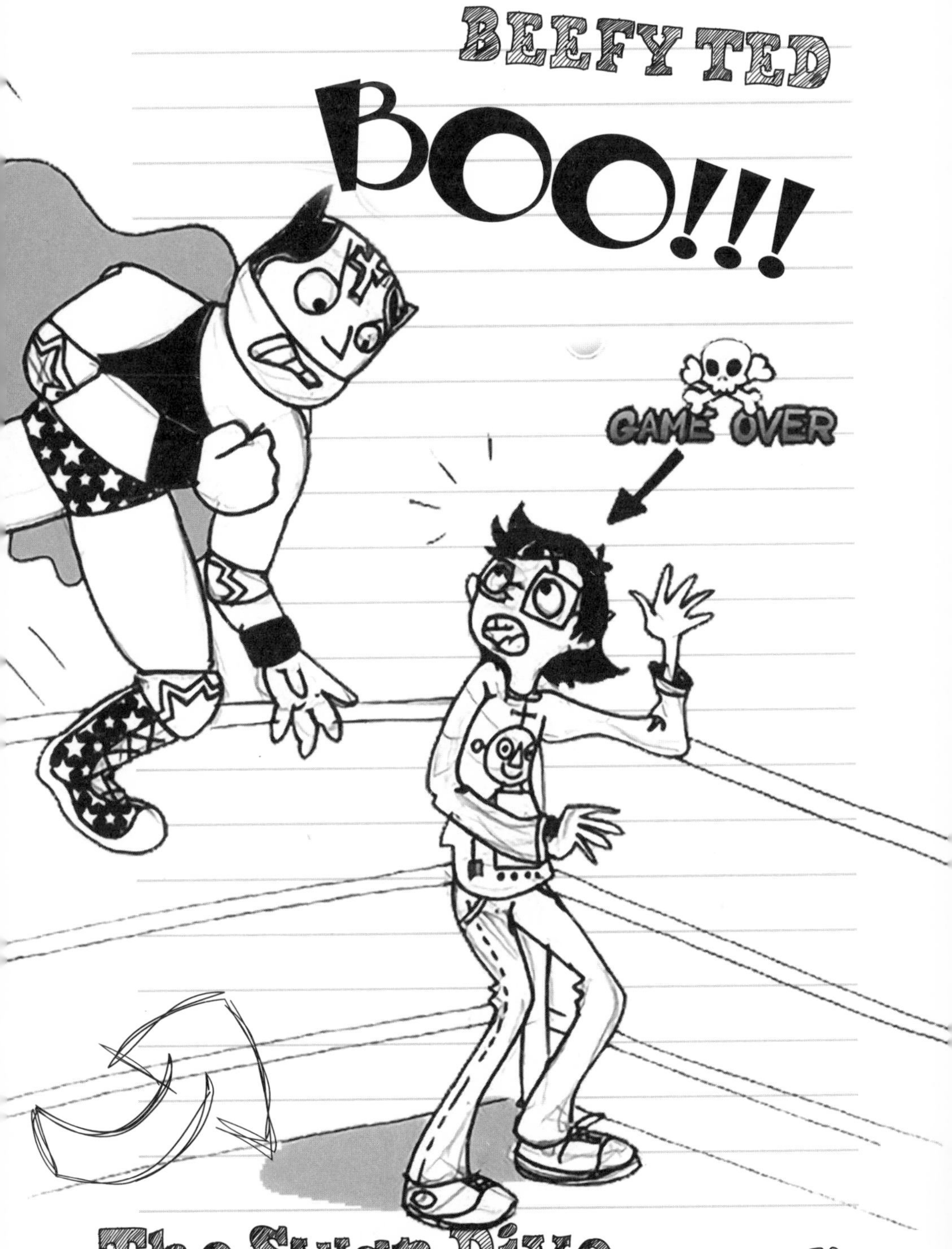

The Swan Dive

Everybody at school knows Ted's nickname is **MYSTERIO!** Guess why? He looks like a **WWE WRESTLER!** I'm sure if he knew I have a crush on Lauren, he would smash me with a swan dive. For months, I've been thinking about him as one of the "**ZOMBIE FARM**" characters. In my nightmares he was **RUNNING** after me to drag me back to the world of the living dead just because I had stared at Lauren.

Short break, in case you don't know what "Zombie Farm" is.

It's a game aimed at training an army made up of zombies with special powers that will allow them to conquer the world in the shortest time! Tired of fighting zombies? GROW them! That's the spirit!

> You've stared at my girl and now you you're going to meet the zombies. Here we watch The Walking Dead JUST to relax!

I was sure she could only fall in love with a brave and athletic guy. I wanted to play my cards right with Lauren and maybe get a chance at payback on one of the bullies.

I gave some serious thought about famous nerd heroes.

All of them have a secret identity! I mean, **PETER PARKER** is not just the brave **Spider-man** climbing up the walls: he's a good student and definitely a bookworm. I don't think his **Instagram** posts would look like this: "DURING THE DAY I'M Peter Parker, A CLUMSY GENIUS, BUT AT NIGHT I'M A SUPERHERO WHO TAKES CARE OF VILLAINS LIKE DOCTOR OCTOPUS."

His enemies wouldn't leave him alone... he'd spend his days deleting his opponents' evil posts! I also studied **DAREDEVIL** comic

books and since the day the world learned **MATT MURDOCK** is **Daredevil** he couldn't lead a normal life. **Poor Matt**, everybody's against him. **FOGGY**, his best friend and partner, had to leave because of the threats he received from Daredevil's enemies. **Every hero has a weak point, that's what the mask is for.**

MIKE WILL BE MY MASK, I want him to have different interests and experiences from mine. He's going to be perfectly custom-made. **HE WILL BE MY OPPOSITE. I love tv shows. HE LOVES SPORTS. I read comic books, MIKE LOVES CYCLING.**

MATT MURDOCK's TROUBLES SINCE EVERYBODY FOUND OUT ABOUT DAREDEVIL

SHORT BREAK: DO YOU KNOW DAREDEVIL? The real Daredevil from Marvel Comics

Daredevil is a famous Marvel superhero. The first issue was published in April 1964. Daredevil was created by writer Stan Lee and artist Bill Everett. He is the alter ego of Matthew "Matt" Murdock, a blind lawyer who grew up in the Hell's Kitchen part of New York City. During the day, he works, as a lawyer defending innocent clients, but at night, he crime as the superhero Daredevil.

I'm a huge STAR WARS fan, he loves **Star Trek**. **NO!** I couldn't. I've put a lot of thought into it and maybe it's **BETTER** Mike doesn't LOVE MOVIES AT ALL! I "liked" some topics on his **Instagram** page, like lots of sports events AND *Justin Bieber*. Don't get me wrong, I can't stand him.

JUSTIN BIEBER

I don't like Justin Bieber. Mike does, but just because he must be my opposite! I'd never walk in his shoes!

Now the only link between me and Mike is **our family.**
I've also published **MY FIRST POST** today: "I'm a **fencing champion** now! Thank you to all of **MY FRIENDS** who turned up at the competition. I love Manhattan and I'll be there to visit my cousin Phil **VERY SOON!**"
I wanted to make the family thing clear for everyone. **I uploaded the picture with the jacket and the trophy.**

The trouble was I had to create **100** fake profiles on **Instagram**! It took me a **LOONG TIME,** but **I needed them!** His **FAKE FOLLOWERS** will make **HIM LOOK REAL** and give him a **credible past.**

I must confess, it **WASN'T EASY OR FAST.**
It took me and my **MAC 5 HOURS**, but finally
MIKE IS REAL! Well, on the web at
least... and if he's alive online, he's definitely
real! Isn't he?

Tomorrow, I'll head to step 2: now that Mike has a **Instagram** profile, I posted and tweeted my compliments to Mike on my personal page so that everyone could see who **Mike was and what he did in his life.** Now each and every

Instagram follower of mine
knows about my cousin.
Including Lauren, obviously.
My perfect plan is set!

MY BRAIN goes on and off, just like Christmas Tree lights!

NOBODY will find out about this little lie and thanks to Mike I'll soon win Lauren's heart. I'm REALLY SATISFIED WITH MY PLAN!

January 13th

I wanted to tell Lauren how cool Mike was and about his victories. She was in the hall next to the lockers, chatting with Kelly. They were laughing like crazy, like they were watching a **Simpsons** episode.

It was the right moment to go to my locker and tell her I went to see Mike's match, letting her know he'd soon be staying with my family for a few days.

I approached her and said: "YOU GIRLS SHOULD MEET MIKE. HE'S COOL. UNFORTUNATELY, I WON'T BE ABLE TO SPEND TIME WITH HIM BECAUSE I'LL BE TRAINING FOR THE MATH TEAM COMPETITION".

Jerk
Arrogant
Tall

TED, the bully

He's always showing his angry face and muscles. I wanted to tell him Mordecai Richler's quote: "It takes 72 muscles to frown, and only 12 to smile. You have to try once."

I didn't get to finish my sentence because Ted came by and loudly said:

"WHAT IS STEPHEN HAWKING'S UGLY BROTHER DOING HERE?"

Ted/Mysterio arrogantly stared at the girls. turned to look at me, daring me to contradict him. I lifted my eyes and realized **I WAS LIKE 6 INCHES** shorter than him... **this was a good reason** to keep my mouth shut. I just wanted to **RUN AWAY,** but I couldn't. That would've put a huge **CHICKEN** mark on my back for the next twenty years.

I was screaming inside: **NOOOOO!**

"I'VE ALWAYS HATED WHEN YOU EGG-HEAD KNOW-IT-ALLS TALK TO MY GIRLFRIEND,"

he said.

"I'M NOT YOUR GIRLFRIEND! I NEVER WAS!" Lauren said in one breath.

HOW WAS THAT POSSIBLE?

Everybody at school knew for a fact they
were together!

**"I HAVE NO INTEREST IN DATING GUYS
WHO BRAG AND USE VIOLENCE JUST TO**

GET NOTICED", she added. Ted's face turned red with anger and threw a punch at my face, but thanks to my fencing training I managed to dodge it. When his fist crashed against the locker, he screamed like a baby.

MY NIGHTMARE!

FORGET ABOUT THE DEATH STAR! PHIL, THE LEGO

Everybody looked at him like the idiot he was, so he turned and left. But not before sentencing me to death. "THIS IS NOT OVER! YOU'D BETTER MOVE TO ANOTHER COUNTRY! YOU'RE NOT SAFE HERE!" I was shaking, but I held my gaze and everybody thought I was brave. Truth is, **I WAS PARALYZED** with fear. Should **I BE MOVING TO PARIS** or try to come to terms with Ted's wrath?

I could never afford a NYC-Paris ticket, so I had to come up with a solution soon, or he would destroy me like a **LEGO** toy.

I got home and logged onto Mike's account before George and Nicholas arrived for the math competition prep. I sent Lauren my friend request and typed a message: "Hi, I'm Phil's cousin. I'll soon be in Mahattan for a fencing competition. My cousin told me great things about you and I'd like to meet you".

After a couple of minutes I was notified: SHE HAD ACCEPETED MY REQUEST. Bingo! Now the plan gets real complicated: I HAD TO TURN MYSELF INTO MY COUSIN MIKE AND MAKE IT SEEM CREDIBLE. HOW COULD I DO THAT?

I would need a partner-in-crime... someone who could help me to plan everything in detail. The only person I could think of was my sister, Ellen. BUT WILL SHE KEEP THE SECRET?

Manhattan ⋯➡

January 14th

I met with Ellen and she **WAS WEARING A REALLY STYLISH DRESS**, as if she was posing for some girls' magazine. I told her about my plan. I was still talking when she suddenly put a piece of paper up to my face:

"With this contract you are willing to lease all the image rights you own to Mike. Sign it, and I'll turn him into the coolest guy ever!

Nothing like you, obviously.

HE will become a star!" she said, all snotty.

sss...secret!!!

"**YOU SCARE ME!**" I answered.

Ellen smirked like she always does when she means "**I'LL DEAL WITH IT**".

I begged her:

"**YOU HAVE TO SWEAR MOM AND DAD WILL NEVER KNOW ABOUT THIS!**"

AM I ELLEN'S OWN FRANKENSTEIN?

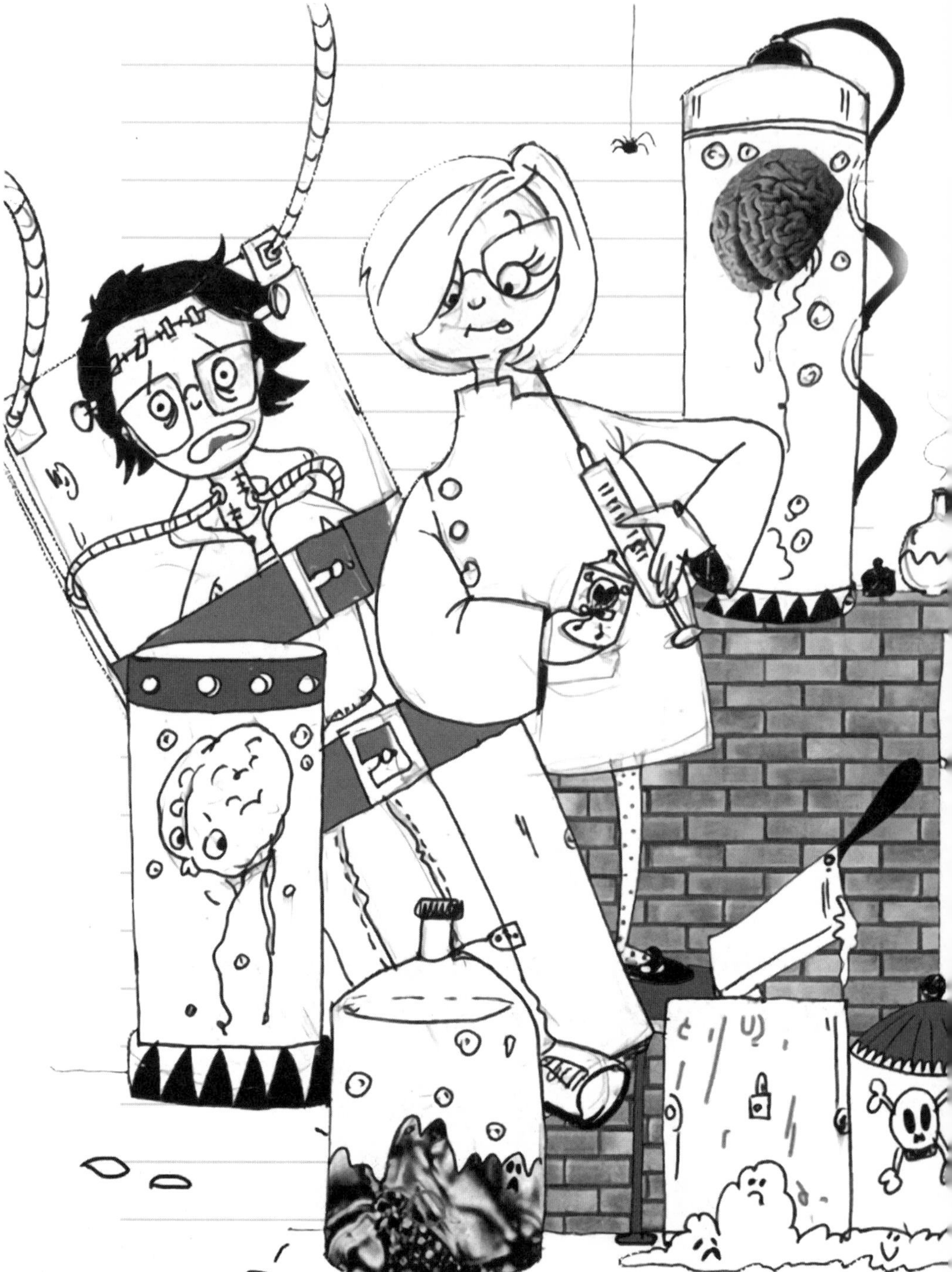

"I WON'T TELL THEM. I WANT TO CREATE MY OWN FRANKENSTEIN!" she sounded like a mad scientist. Now I'm in my sister's hands...

OH BOY.

January 15th

George came by after school holding the competition schedule. Nicholas wisely suggested we should start training, so Ellen started filming us for a documentary she is directing titled "The Ping Pong Theory". She wants to shoot a movie about NERDS and their weird hobbies. WE MET IN MY BEDROOM WITH ALL OF OUR DEVICES AND NOTEPADS. We looked like warriors ready for battle. "I WANT TO FILM NERDS HAVING THE TIME OF THEIR LIVES DOING MATH TESTS!", Ellen said, her voice filled with sarcasm.

"YOU SHOULD MIND YOUR OWN BUSINESS! LOOK AT YOU: YOU'RE EIGHT AND ALL YOU DO IS SPEND YOUR ALLOWANCE ON SOCIAL MEDIA!"

a vexed **GEORGE** replied. Nicholas hardly speaks, but he always giggled when **ELLEN** and George fought.

"I DO THE SAME THINGS ALL THE GIRLS MY AGE DO! I PLAY Barbie AND Cooking Mama JUST LIKE THE OTHER GIRLS!"

"Sure." George said. "Stop it, you two. If we really want to win this thing we have to stick together and train seriously".

Dear Diary, we started doing exercises at 5. Ellen's mobile phone stopwatch started ticking. The more time passed by, the more anxious we became. We couldn't focus. Even the simplest exercise was tough due to time pressure.

"PHIL AND NICHOLAS, THIS IS TERRIBLE! AND GEORGE, WELL, YOU'RE THE WORST!" Ellen yelled. "GUYS, GET A HOLD OF YOUSELVES OR YOU'LL PANIC! YOU'LL NEVER WIN!"

"Okay, genius, any ideas?" asked George.

Ellen wanted to improve our

psychomotor performance so she took us to

the park and we decided to **FOLLOW HER INSTRUCTIONS.**

She drew a line on the ground and we were supposed to walk straight on it, while balancing some books on our heads.

She was filming the whole thing and yelling at us. She was definitely having a great time.

We looked like three idiots repeating math formulas, walking on a thin line with books on our heads.

We made plenty of mistakes and we felt **NERVOUS** because we all felt very stupid.

At the end of the training though, the books were not falling anymore and **OUR HEARTS WEREN'T POUNDING LIKE CRAZY.** Long story short, we had learned how to handle **extreme pressure!**

I'M NOT YOUR CREATURE

Ellen was as happy as if she had created three new Edward Scissorhands. The world was her lab and she was the scientist creating her own creatures!

January 17th

I saw Lauren at school and she looked more beautiful than ever.

She has everything I love: she's got Amanda's smile from REVENGE, Penny's positivity from **The Big Bang Theory** and Phoenix's hair. SHE WAS THE PERFECT MIX, she was a dream. She was like my MARY JANE to PETER PARKER.

And to me, she was like the last flick of the Rubik's cube, the one leading to happiness. She gave me her standard, plain smile. She was just being NORMAL. WHY?!?!

Why wasn't she looking at me differently? "Your cousin Mike is getting into town tomorrow", she said after a while. I FELT EMBARRASSED.

I was shaking, but I thought about Ellen's exercises and stopped panicking.

"YEAH... RIGHT!"

HER HAIR IS LIKE X-MEN's PHOENIX

"HE ASKED ME OUT," she added.

"Oh? Well, **that would be a great help! I'm studying hard for the math competition**," I told her.

"OH, YEAH. RIGHT. THAT'S WHAT YOU BRAINIACS DO."

That's what I was to her: nothing but a brainiac.

"IT'S LIKE A FOOTBALL GAME. OR A RUGBY MATCH. IT'S A COMPETITION. PEOPLE WATCH THEM BECAUSE THERE'S A WINNER AND A LOSER".

Lauren looked interested, but she was just being polite. Probably because she didn't have the slighest interest in math. She was wearing a **KATY PERRY** t-shirt and I'm sure she thought I was boring.

But tomorrow I'll have

 and I'll sort things

out... thanks to Mike!

NOTHING BUT A BRAINIAC!

PHIL THE WATCHER

AM I A BRAINIAC?

AM I REALLY LIKE MARVEL'S THE WATCHER?

January 19th

Skip day!

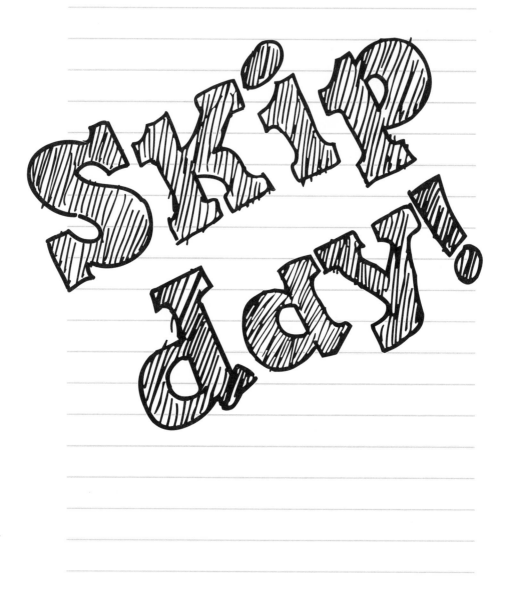

January 20th

Lauren looked amazing and I was so **SCARED**.

Ellen put some blush on my cheeks, **FIXED MY HAIR WITH GEL AND DREW A MOLE ON MY FACE. I was ready to meet Lauren!**

MY HEART WAS BEATING FAST because I'm not very good at lying, but I felt like an actor in that moment and I had to play my role properly. **I LOWERED MY VOICE A LITTLE AND IT SOUNDED MORE DETERMINED, LESS SCARED THAN USUAL.**

I had spent all night thinking about how to change my typical gestures so she wouldn't realize that **Phil and Mike were the exact same person**. Ellen was clever enough to take away my **STAR WARS** hoodie and insisted I wear a much cooler shirt.

105

MY SISTER HAD TAKEN CARE OF EVERY DETAIL.

She had also bought some leather wristbands to make me look cooler. **I gathered my courage and I went to go see Lauren.** She was waiting for me outside. It was raining and we were both holding our umbrellas while her father was moving the car. He had parked quite close and was heading to a shop nearby. I didn't have a lot of time and I had to use every second of those 60 minutes.

She was staring at me with her big eyes.

"DO I LOOK LIKE PHIL? EVERYBODY SAYS SO!" I told her. She smiled. "YOU LOOK BETTER."

"Why?"

"YOU LOOK VERY CONFIDENT. Well, the mole... that messy hair, the wristbands...Mmm... YOU LOOK A BIT LIKE HIM, BUT YOU LOOK..."

106

"I look...?" I asked, hoping she'd say something good about me.

"You look like a normal guy."

I didn't know whether that was a compliment or not. Anyway, I smiled at her.

We walked for a bit then sat at a table at McDonald's while her father was running errands. SHE TOOK MY HAND. My other hand was shaking and I HAD TO FIGHT HARD NOT TO DROP MY COKE. Lauren told me she loved one of my wristbands, so I took it off and gave it to her. Her eyes looked heart-shaped and I felt like I had just climbed up Mount Everest. The only thing missing was some romantic music. That all changed in a second when TED ENTERED MCDONALD'S.

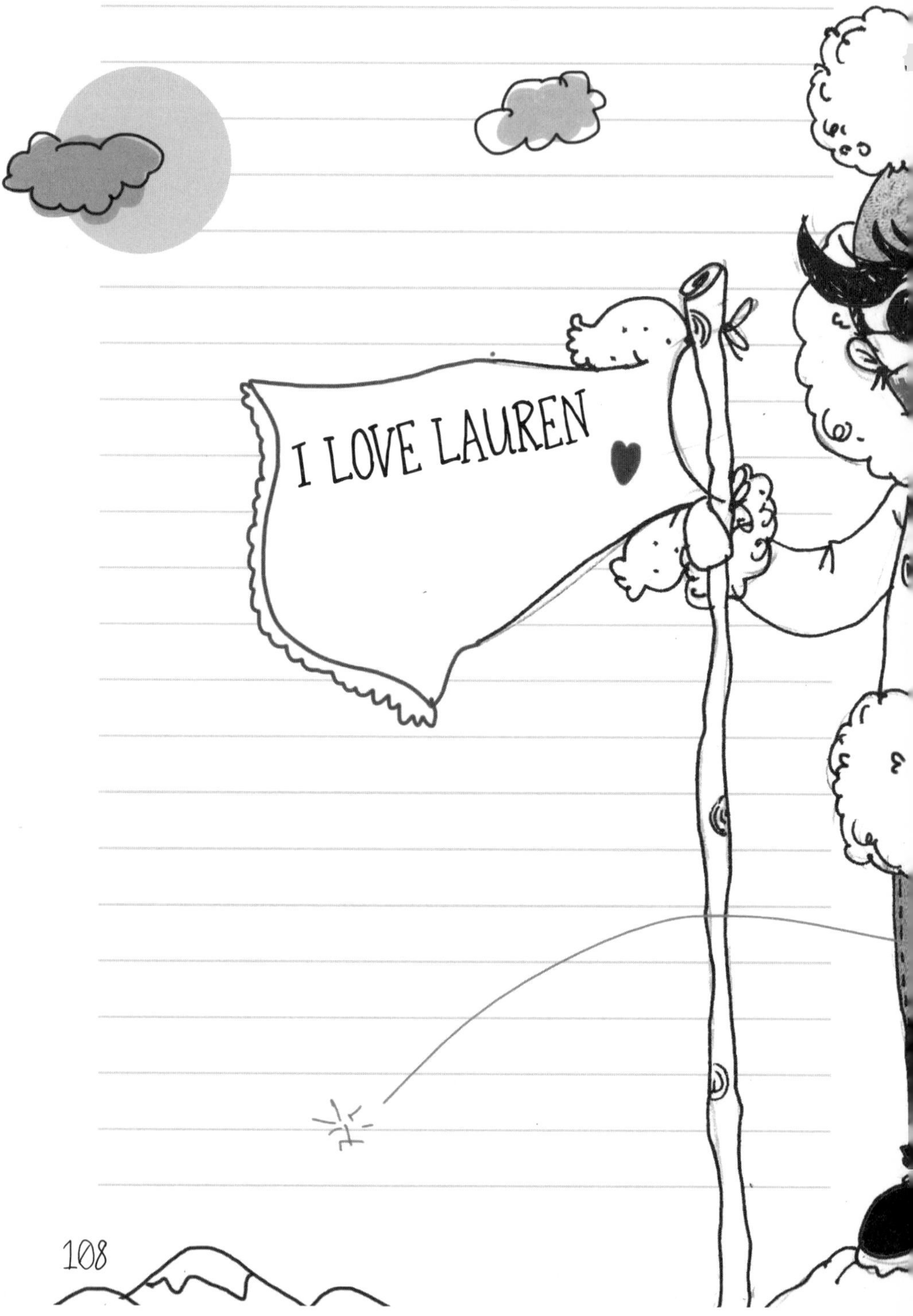
I LOVE LAUREN

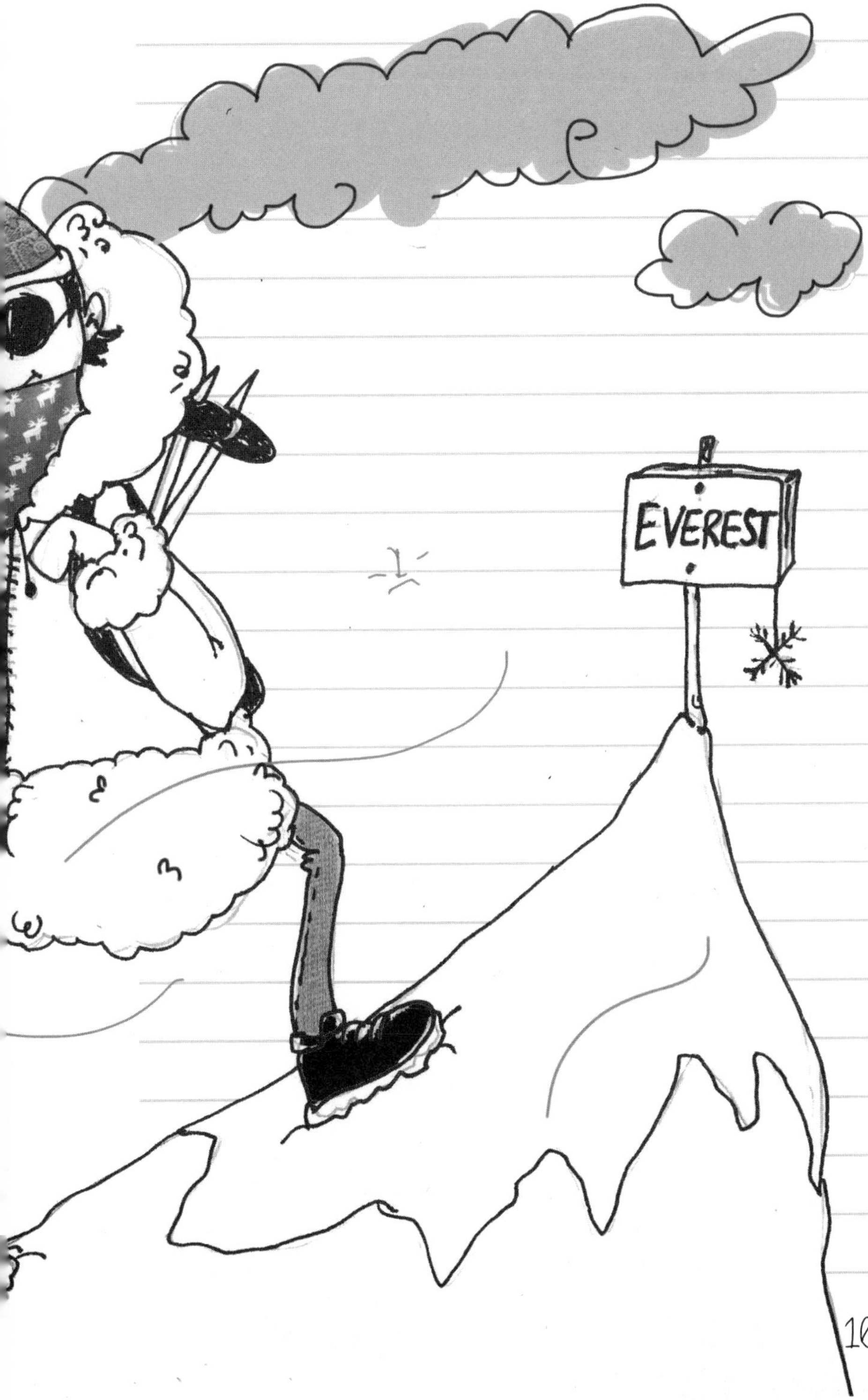
EVEREST

I imagine if Wolverine had found out his claws were nothing but plastic, he would've felt the same as I did.

I was hoping he wouldn't see me, but he found us in a second and immediately came over. **MY LEGS WERE SHAKING UNDER THE TABLE.**

"Phil! Phil the Nerd with my girlfriend! Again!!!" he screamed. "IT'S MIKE, IT'S PHIL'S COUSIN!" Lauren said. "Hey you, idiot, what's happening?" I asked with an attitude I didn't know I had. "AS FAR AS I KNOW, SHE'S NOT YOUR GIRLFRIEND AND I'M NO NERD. THAT'S TWO MISTAKES IN ONE SENTENCE."

Ted was smiling like Doctor Doom does... and that wasn't a GOOD SIGN! MY JOKE hadn't really softened his mood, clearly. "You're a bad imitation of a terrible original!" he growled while throwing a punch at me.

Everybody in the room was staring.

I jumped back to dodge it and saw a couple of UMBRELLAS NOT FAR FROM ME. I grabbed one and aimed it right at his head. When he saw that, he immediately seized the other umbrella and tried to hit me. **I jumped into the air and hit him on the shoulder so I wouldn't hurt him too bad.**

"Mr. Wrestling" fought back, but I blocked and hit him with a strike on the hand (or "quinte", as we say in fencing). HIS UMBRELLA FELL DOWN ON THE FLOOR AND HE GOT SCARED. ONE OF THE EMPLOYEES PUSHED US QUITE ABRUPTLY TO THE EXIT. LAUREN WAS ASTONISHED.

She was charmed because I was so bold and fierce! BUT DON'T GET ME WRONG, I WASN'T HAPPY.

I had only been Mike for a couple of hours. I got into a fight and told a billion lies.

This was more than I had **ever done in 12 years as myself**. And I felt guilty, **even if LAUREN was falling for me.**

THAT'S HIM! TED DOOM!

January 26th

Dear Diary, tomorrow is the day of the math competition! Today the team met at my place and we couldn't contain our excitement !
"I CAN'T WAIT TO TAKE DOWN ALL THOSE FIFTH GRADERS, BUT I NEED YOUR HELP."
George told me.
"WE'RE ALMOST THERE, WE HAVE TO WIN,"
Nicholas added.
"PHIL, YOU'LL HAVE TO STUDY. YOU'RE NOT READY YET" said Ellen.
"DISTRACTIONS WON'T BE ALLOWED," George added. I was REALLY distracted, though ! I kept on checking my phone and when I finally got a note on Mike's Messenger I felt so relieved I smiled and all the worry disappeared in a second.

"ABOUT YESTERDAY... YOU'RE MY HERO!" I was still feeling guilty about what I had done to Ted, but I refused to think about it.

"Want to meet?" she asked me after a few seconds.

"Sure," I answered, even though I was

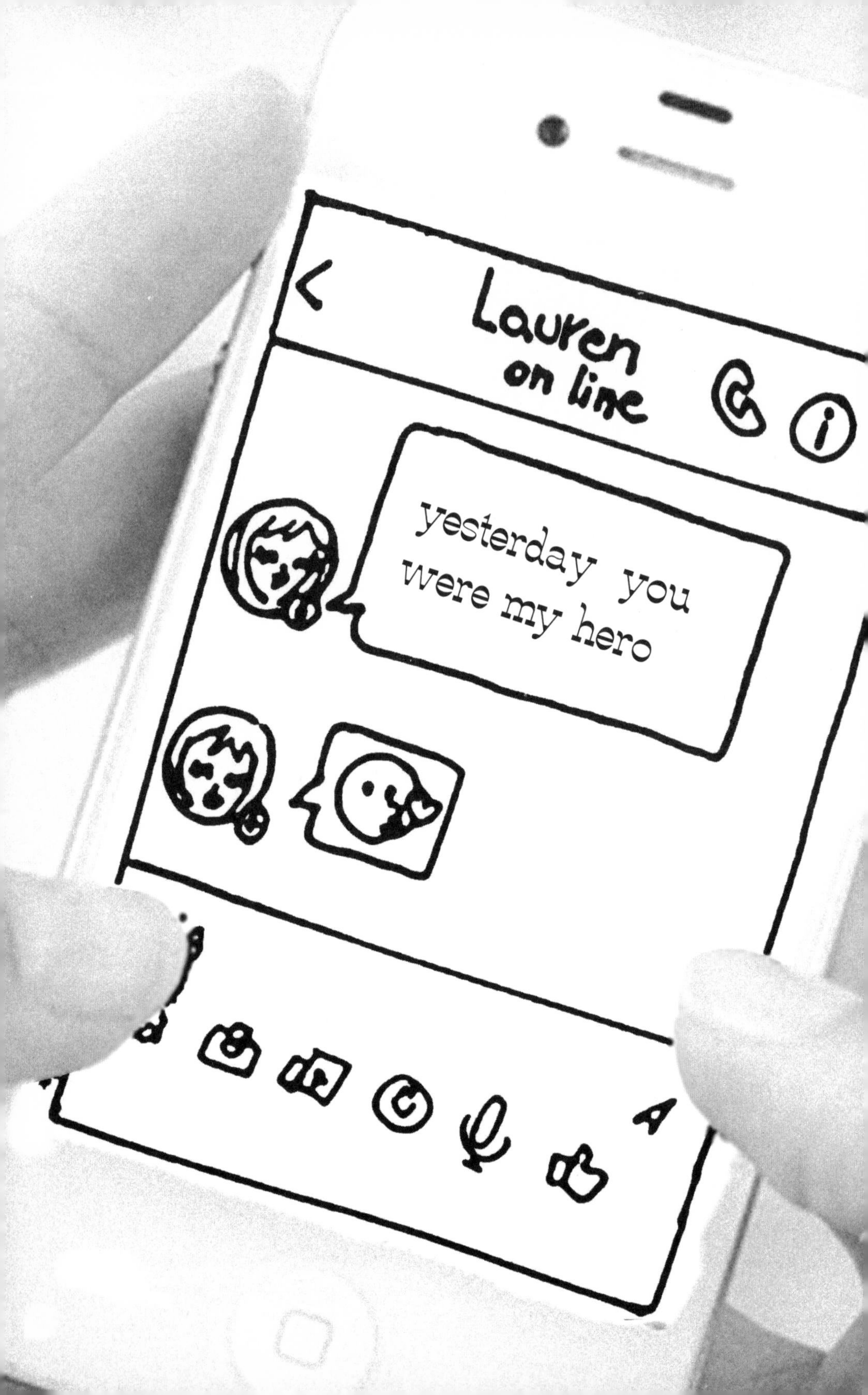
Lauren
on line
yesterday you were my hero

well aware of the fact I couldn't. Would I lie to my team just to see her?

"Guys, you get started...I'll be back in an hour or so...".

"WHERE ARE YOU GOING?"

"I have to pick up a book I bought from Amazon. The postman wasn't able to drop it off and I don't want them to send it back, so I'll just walk down to the post office and get it myself." I explained.

ONE MORE LIE! I had lied to my sister and my best friends. I was an idiot. I felt guilty, but I wanted to see Lauren. One thing was clear to me:

A STORM WAS COMING.

PHIL'S NOTE:

To cut things short, wanna know what happened later? I met Lauren after putting my "disguise" in the elevator. This is how **Clark Kent** must feel when he turns into **Superman** in a phone booth! She started talking about music I don't really like, but I pretended I loved an **Ariana Grande** song, just to look more appealing: **LIE # 1.** **LIE # 2**: I finally found an excuse so I could sneak back to my friends.

118

On the way back home, I spent all my money at the BOOK STORE next to my apartment building because I needed a book to show my friends, otherwise they'd have found out **i HAD BEEN LYING TO THEM JUST TO MEET LAUREN.**

I looked for something interesting, but time was running out, so I just grabbed the first book from a pile. It looked like it was about math, **"THE REVELATION NUMBERS."** Before going back to **George, Nicholas** and **Ellen** I passed by the kitchen to greet my parents and my dad asked me about my recent trip to the book store because he had seen me.

I ANSWERED AND *I LIED*, again.

"I met a friend from school named Mike." WHEN I WENT BACK, ALL MY FRIENDS WERE ANGRY. I couldn't keep up with all those lies. I just wanted to start things all over again, but the lies were like an avalanche I couldn't control anymore.

January 27th

Today was competition day!

How did it go?

Well, every mathematician and physicist in town is literally **TERRIFIED of Big Mind Kill!** She's every **Stephen Hawking** aspirant's worst nightmare! People tell the most incredible stories about her... she's got a real name, but no one remembers it, nor dares to speak it! **SHE'S A LEGEND. HER NICKNAME'S BIG MIND KILL BECAUSE SHE CAN CONTROL BRAINS.** They say she's got real superpowers.

Don't laugh at me, dear Diary... she's really something special.

BIG
MIND
KILL

TERRIBLE

BIG MIND KILL LEGEND!

EVERY FORMER OPPONENT IN THE PREVIOUS MATCHES SAID IT'S JUST IMPOSSIBLE TO BEAT HER DUE TO HER SUPERPOWERS.

Apparently, she's got a sort of psychic power that allows her to create a magnetic beam clouding the enemy's mind! **Do you believe these stories? Me neither.** Still, everybody says she really does have some superhuman abilities! Legend has it that she managed to beat chess champion Garry Kasparov the **FIRST** time she played the game. **THIS IS BIG MIND KILL.** I mean, her background speaks for itself: **SHE WAS A THREE-TIME FINALIST AT THE MATH COMPETITION.** Want to know how many victories she has had?

Three out of three. No one was ever able to fight her magnetic field. Even the professor asking the questions during the competition forgot everything he was supposed to ask her!

Big Mind Kill is beautiful and mysterious. She's always wrapped up in her coat and hides her hair with a wool hat.

She came up to me, and trust me, **TED THE BULLY** would've been ten times more pleasant!

She said: "MAY THE BEST MAN WIN! WILL i SEE YOU iN THE FiNALS?" I didn't know what to say. She had **beautiful eyes,** but they were creepy somehow. **I was so scared.** Ellen ran over and immediately replied: "HONEY, FORGET ABOUT THE FiNALS iF YOU COME UP AGAiNST MY TEAM!" I'd have loved to shut my sister up, but didn't want to hurt her feelings in front of all of those people.

BIG MIND KILL

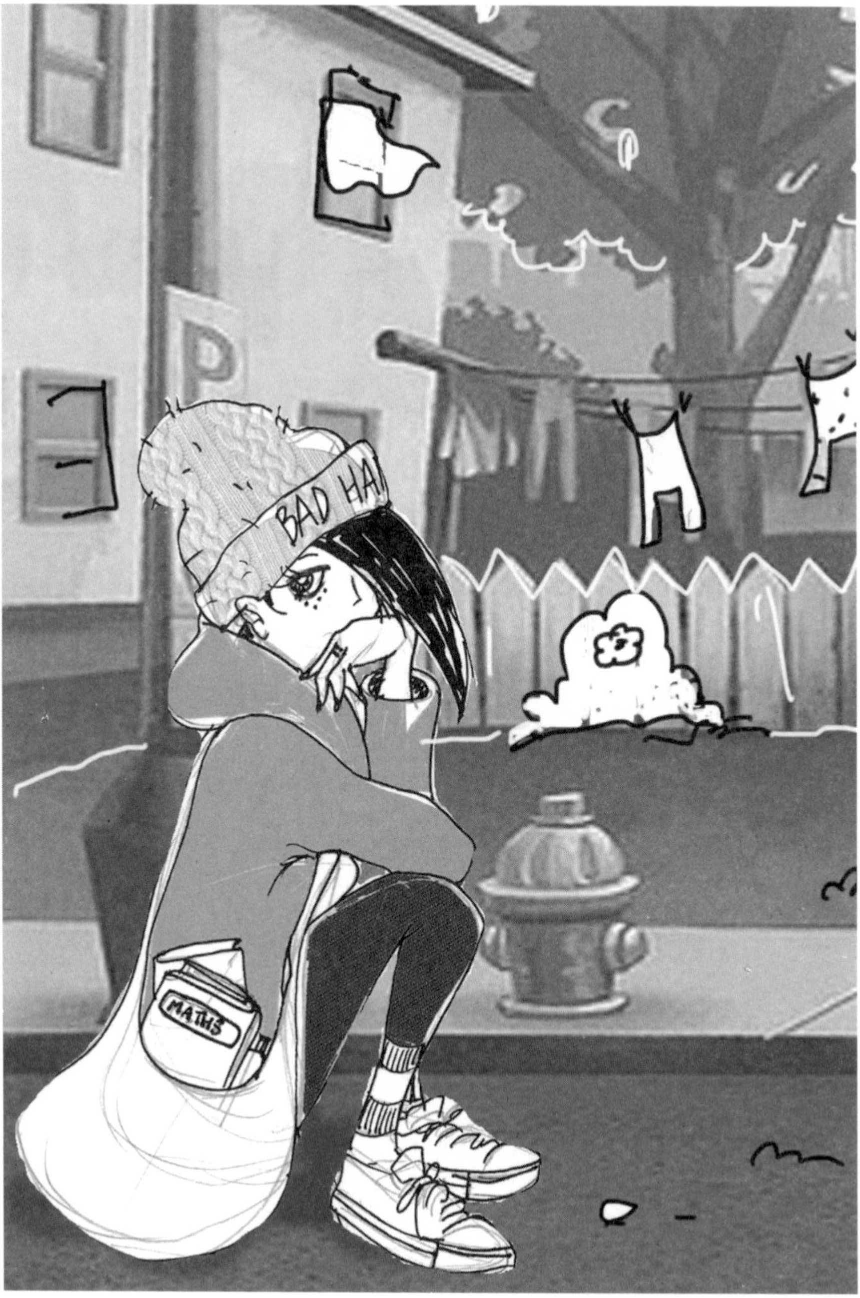
BAD HA
MATHS

OUR TEAM WILL WIN!

DO YOU REALLY THINK I'M SCARED OF BIG MIND KILL?

Nicholas put his paper bag on his head and **George** wanted to look prepared, so he walked by murmuring: "Guys, I did it. A^x+ B^y = C^z. That's a piece of cake!" EVERYBODY LOOKED AT HIM LIKE HE HAD GONE MENTAL.

The competiton finally started and we met "The **Goonies**": NOTHING BUT NERDS, just like us. BECAUSE OF THE MOVIE FROM 1985 BY RICHARD DONNER and **Steven Spielberg**.

The movie's about some kids who grew up in the "**boondocks**" of Astoria, Oregon. The "boondocks" aren't the nicest parts of the town. So the guys jokingly called their neighborhood "**the Goon docks**".

And that is why they called themselves the "**Goonies.**"

THE MOVIE CHARACTERS WERE SUPERCOOL, BUT OUR OPPONENTS IN THE MATH COMPETITION WERE JUST PATHETIC. They were nothing but a bunch of 4th graders wearing huge glasses and fake gold teeth that were supposed to look threatening.

We were called **The Ping Pong Theory**.

Our name was an **IRONIC TRIBUTE** to **our favorite tv series.**

Mark was the **Goonies** captain because he was the oldest. He told me: "**I REALLY HOPE THEY'RE GOING TO ASK US ABOUT MAXWELL EQUATIONS, YOU KNOW, ELECTROMAGNETISM. WE'RE THE BEST PREPARED EXPERTS IN AMERICA.**"

Ellem screamed, "HEY, YOU SNOTTY-KID, IF YOUR BRAIN HAD JUST A TENTH OF MY BROTHER'S CAPACITY, YOU WOULD BE GETTING YOUR NOBEL PRIZE BY NOW!"

"If you want war...I'll give it to you!" Mark replied.

If I had a giant slingshot, **I'D HAVE SENT ELLEN TO ANOTHER CITY, POSSIBLY ANOTHER COUNTRY!** Maybe South Dakota so she could go to **Mount Rushmore** and welcome all the **tourists**.

We were about to start. **Professor Zemeckis** walked in and our jaws dropped.

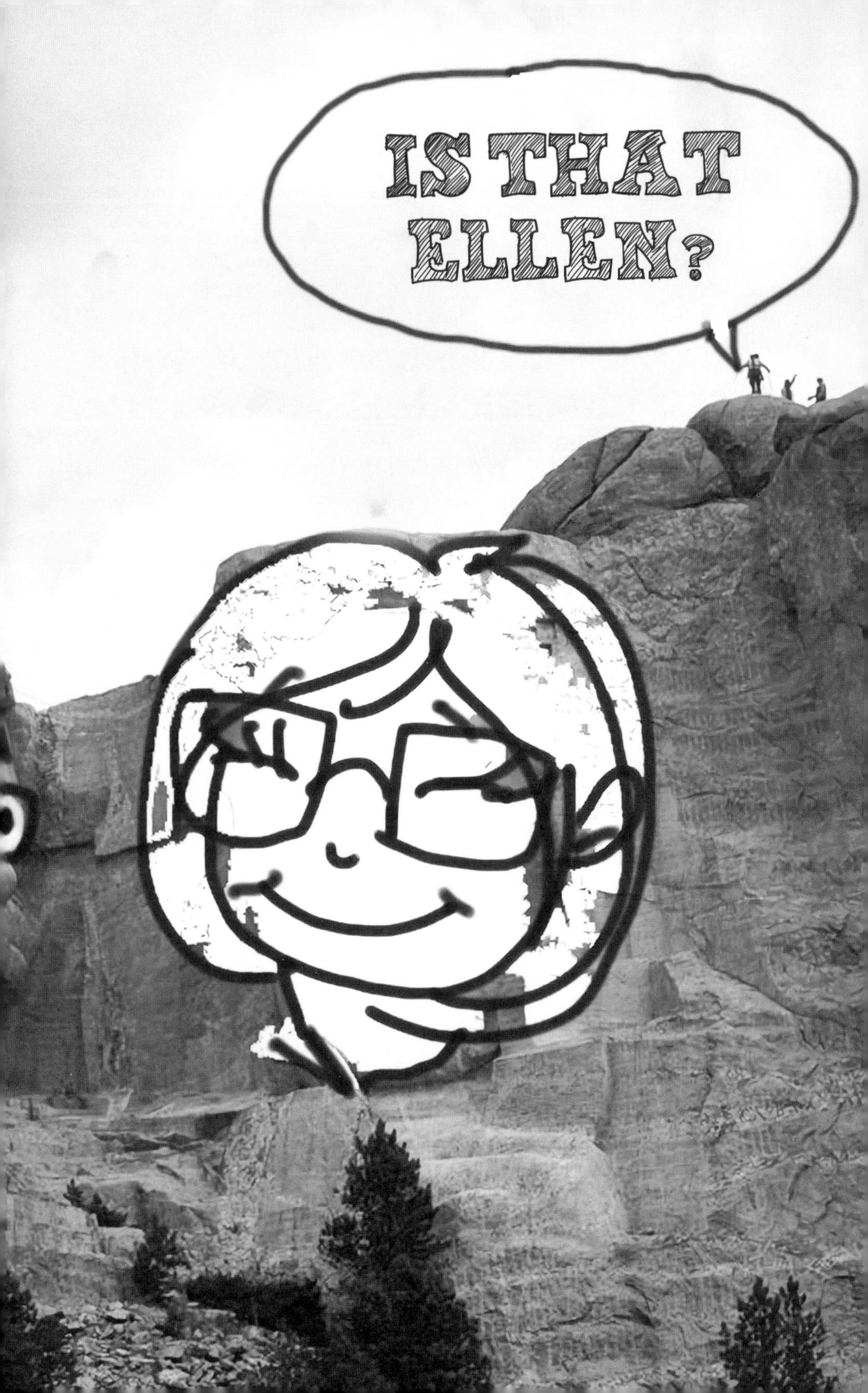
IS THAT ELLEN?

He looked like **Doc Brown** from **Back to The Future**, the only thing that was missing was a **DeLorean.**

ELLEN REMINDED US TO FOCUS AND NOT TO LET OUR METAPHORICAL BOOKS FALL FROM OUR HEADS.

George couldn't stop biting his nails.

Nicholas was silent, no paper bag on his head.

Do you want to know how the FIRST match went?

Professor Zemeckis introduced the first subject. I was hoping it would turn out being Quantum physics, but instead it was Faraday's Law about electromagnetism. I realized the **Goonies** would win this round. But, George stayed positive and while we were reading our question, he calmly said : "WE'RE HANDING IN OUR PAPERS IN 2 MINUTES."

"HOW'S THAT POSSIBLE?"

Nicholas asked. "Faraday's Law describes Faraday's law of induction which is a basic law of electromagnetism predicting how a magnetic field will interact with an electric circuit to produce an electromotive force: a phenomenon called electromagnetic induction. I know that because I dreamt about him yesterday!"

"**GREAT!**" I screamed. We filled the answer in and handed everything in in less than 90 seconds.

The Goonies were destroyed and there was really no competition! That was such a blast! So we reached the **ROUND OF 16** where we met the DOCTOR WHO TEAM. They were **BRITISH** and were all wearing the same suit, including **horrible ties**. They looked completely emotionless.

They were so stiff and **snobbish that** they didn't even realize the competiton had started. **Nicholas was able to solve the chemistry question** about Lewis' Theory in less than 30 seconds. When they lost, all they said was: "Still, **The Beatles** were **BRITISH**, anyway." **THEIR PERFORMANCE ENDED AS SHAMEFULLY AS IT HAD BEGUN.** The **DOCTOR WHO TEAM** got their

DOCTOR WHO TEAM BRITISH

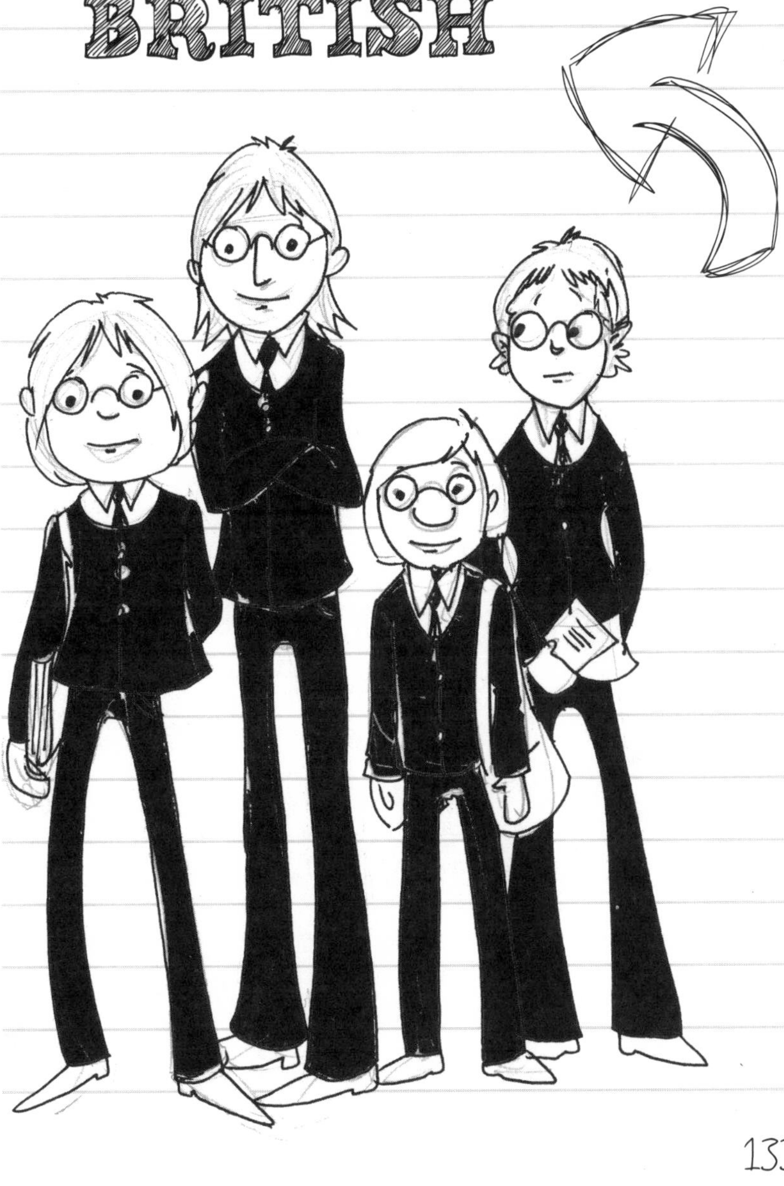

inspiration from the British sci-fi TV series **Doctor Who**, produced by the **BBC SINCE 1963**. I suppose they went straight home by **TARDIS**: a time and space machine that works through the time vortex. Now, we were in **QUARTER-FINALS** against **the Vampire Diaries. THEY WERE REALLY EVIL AND CRUEL. They faked legal documents and had a 60 year old man on their team.** He was wearing tons of make-up to look like a teenager. **THEY WERE THE WORST OPPONENTS EVER.**

They drew their inspiration from the **HORROR TV SERIES** created by **KEVIN WILLIAMSON** and **JULIE PLEC** based on **L.J. Smith's** book series. They were wearing some absurd capes, but what really **SCARED ME WERE** the dark circles around their eyes.

THE VAMPIRE DIARIES

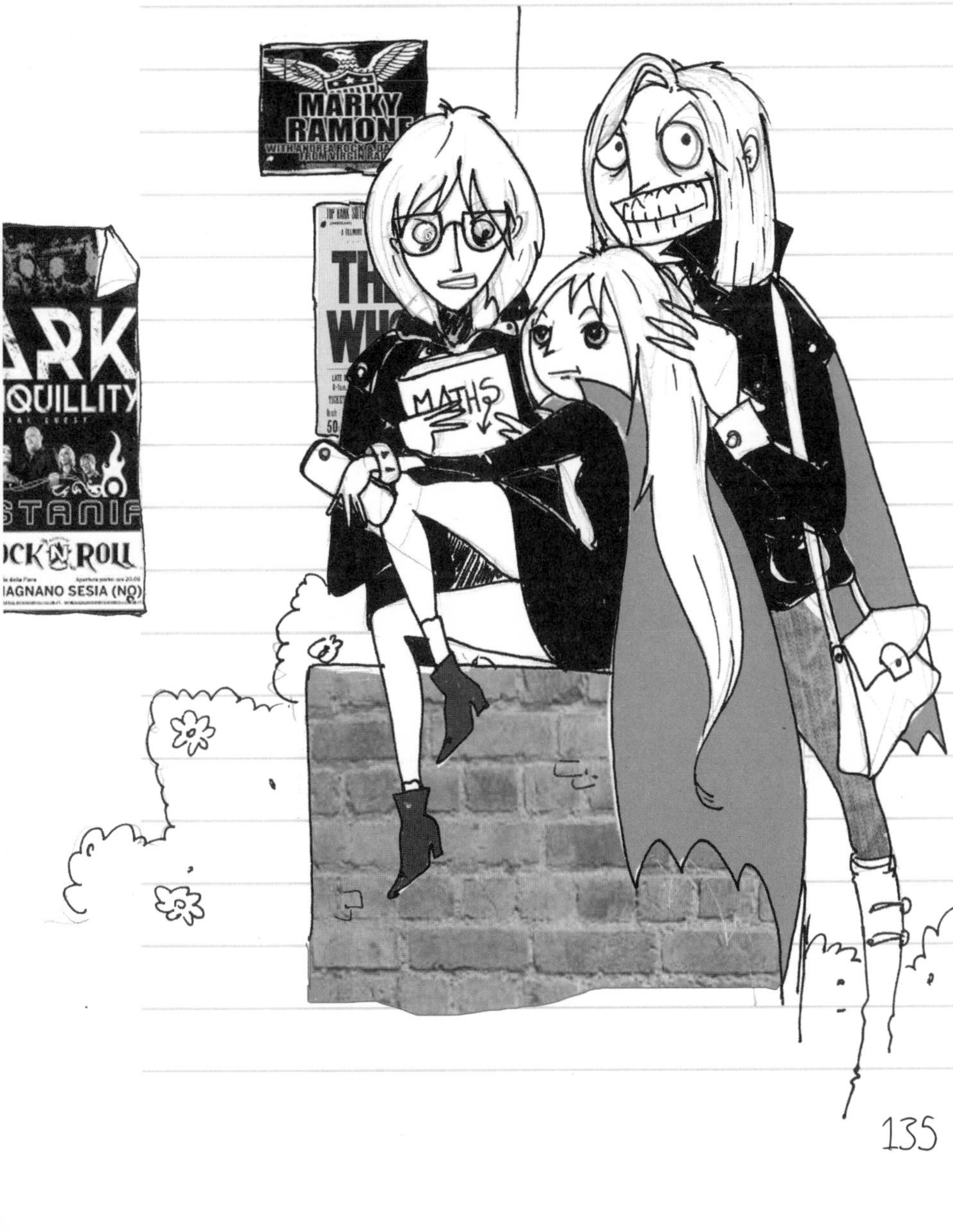
MARKY RAMONE
MATHS

THEY WERE REALLY RUTHLESS: they used

a computer during the test without **Prof. Zemeckis** noticing it and tried to copy our notes right in front of our faces! The test was about **MAX PLANCK** and the electromagnetic waves. **I managed to solve each and every problem easily in the shortest time,** and we won!

Now we were in the Semifinals against

the ONE DIRECTION MENTALIST TEAM.

They were nothing to laugh about! They really looked like **One Direction**.

They also had a huge bunch of screaming girls supporting them. **THEY WERE THE MOST POPULAR GUYS IN THEIR SCHOOL AND EVERYBODY CHEERED FOR THEM.**

Harry was the team captain and looked exactly **like Harry Styles.** His agent was even giving him the right answers. When I asked Professor Zemeckis why they had been allowed to have a prompter, he simply told me: "**Thanks to that team, we had the money to sponsor this event!**"

Beating them wasn't going to be a walk in the park... **THEY DIDN'T CARE ABOUT THE RULES AND EVERYBODY WAS ROOTING FOR THEM.** The next question was about identifying shapes in space and using them to solve geometry problems. **THE TEAM'S AGENTS CALLED IN AN EXPERT!** That was so unfair! If they could count on this extra help, we were going to lose miserably. **Luckily, my sister had a great idea:** she used her **FREQUENCY JAMMER TO BLOCK ALL SIGNALS,** so no one in the room was able to use any kind of electronic device... **THIS ALLOWED US TO FINISH THE PROBLEM IN NO TIME AND MOVE ON TO THE FINALS!**

FREQUENCY JAMMER! (ELLEN'S IDEA)

THE OTHER FINALISTS were none other than *Big Mind Kill's* team, THE KILLER MINDS:

THE FINAL MATCH WILL BE IN TWO DAYS. We are terribly scared, but ready... for the worst!

This is George Lucas!

January 28th

Today was **the day of the national fencing competition.** I had to forget about Phil and get into Mike's clothes. I didn't tell Mom either 'cause **i DIDN'T WANT HER TO TALK TO HER FRIENDS.** No one knew about the match except Lauren, but **I was sure she wouldn't be interested in watching me! SORRY: iN WATCHING MIKE.** In the morning, she sent me an email where she said she loved my taste in music, my attitude, my athleticism and the way I dressed, **SHE WAS BASICALLY ATTRACTED TO SOMEONE WHO DIDN'T EXIST,** 'cause I was Phil and I couldn't pretend I was Mike forever.

BUT *I REALLY LIKED HER...* so I replied and told her I wanted her close to me on that special day. I never thought she would come to **watch me fence!** **Especially since her mom said she couldn't...**

When Karen, Lauren's mom, realized that the pillows and blankets watching tv at home were not her daughter, **SHE IMMEDIATELY RAN TO MY PARENTS' HOUSE.**

Why did she go to my parents? Because according to

Mike's email on Lauren's computer, he was staying at my place! Lauren's mom knew where my family lived, so she **got there quickly**. I still didn't know that **MY VOLCANO OF LIES** was ready to **ERUPT!**

Mom was drawing and she

was so focused, she didn't hear the doorbell ringing like crazy. **As SOON As KAREN GOT IN, SHE STARTED ASKING QUESTIONS ABOUT MIKE.** She wanted to know everything. **Obviously my mom had no clue who Mike was.**

I'M KAREN, LAUREN'S MOTHER!

WHO IS IT?

They were both wondering about who **MIKE MIGHT BE**... Mom started connecting the dots, just like she does when drawing, so she realized I had been lying about Mike and the book.

"My son went shopping for books with a guy named Mike... I want to know what's going on! Is he in trouble?"

My favorite illustrator.

THE BOOK

Mom ran to my bedroom and grabbed the book I had bought. When she read the title "**The Revelation Numbers**" she was shocked:

it looked like a math book, **BUT IT WAS NOT** about math. Instead, it was about the end of the world, written by **a CRAZY writer. WELL, I'LL ADMIT IT... IT DIDN'T LOOK VERY REASSURING.** "**What kind of people are they hanging out with!**" she almost screamed. "**LET'S CALL THE POLICE!**" Karen suggested.

A couple of minutes later, Ray arrived at my place: he's a **policeman** who lived nearby. He picked them up and headed to the arena where the fencing competition was held. **They wanted to ask me a couple of things.**

Dear *Diary*, are you wondering about what Dad was doing at this time? I'm telling you: **NOTHING.** He didn't know anything. He was still clinging to his telescope, hoping to see some UFOS.

In the meantime, I was fighting against my opponent wearing Mike's jacket and **a mask hiding my face**.

I was one of the FINALISTS.

I was a strong opponent because fencing was easy to me, just like playing with physics or numbers. LAUREN WAS ALMOST PASSING OUT FROM ALL THE SCREAMING AND ADMIRATION.

She really made me feel confident. **I was winning 8 to 2 in the epée competition,** which is a great score considering you only need 10 to win!

In a nutshell, I was thrashing him and he'd never be able to claw back from such a score.

I was two thrusts from victory and THE TITLE OF NATIONAL CHAMPION.

That's when Ray walked in and went straight

to the judges, **asking for the match to be suspended.** I was **SHOCKED** and didn't realize what was going on. APPARENTLY, CHAOS HAD TAKEN OVER MY WHOLE LIFE AFTER THE BILLIONS OF LIES I'D BEEN TELLING.

The policeman asked me to take off my mask.

"**But, that's Phil!**" my mom screamed.

"**No! That's Phil's cousin!**" Lauren screamed back at her, astonished.

"**Which cousin?**" Mom asked.

The judges asked what my name was and I admitted "**PHIL. I'M PHIL THE NERD.**" I was very sad.

Well, long story short, **I RECEIVED THE BLACK CARD** and was **DISQUALIFIED.** I had faked my identity and that was a violation.

"**NOOOOOOOO!!!**"

I was a few steps away from the title...

I put my glasses on and went to Lauren. The mole had disappeared from sweat during the match. She stared at me a bit and then said:

"**Really? A nerd?**

I had a crush on a nerd?! NO WAY!"

WELL, THAT WAS WHEN LAUREN WALKED OUT OF THE BUILDING... AND OUT OF MY LIFE.

Want to know what happened during the math competition finals? Relax. Calm down. THE AVALANCHE EFFECT OF ALL MY LIES didn't only involve fencing: when my friends heard

My name is Phil, Phil the nerd

LAUREN

about the whole drama they felt betrayed and didn't want to speak to me anymore. I was the first one to believe in our nerd clan...

and the FIRST to betray everyone with my useless lies!

Lies can be very dangerous.

¡ HATE LiES!

HI, I KNOW A LIAR GUY. BUT THAT'S ANOTHER STORY!

The only way to FiX THiNGS is to stop adding lies on top of the rest.

January 29th

The day of the finals, neither **George** nor Nicholas turned up on time. I didn't know if they decided to forgive me. I had bought **STAR WARS** action figures for **Nicholas** and George and a subscription to FORBES for Ellen.

I didn't know whether they were going to come or not, but I just wanted to be forgiven. **I COULDN'T BELIEVE MY EYES WHEN I SAW THE THREE OF THEM FINALLY WALKING IN!** They looked so much like the cast of **Armageddon**, I was almost hearing Aerosmith playing in the background!
They were smiling and looked happy. When I gave them their presents, they hugged me. **THEY HAD NO HARD FEELINGS AND JUST WANTED TO WIN THE CUP!**
"**I'm sorry guys. I did it because of Lauren. I was crazy for her.**" I explained.
"We felt sorry for you! Turning yourself into someone else just to be loved, it doesn't make any sense!" George said.
Ellen looked very sad. I hugged my little sister and said: "I swear, I won't be telling **ANY MORE** lies from now on... and now let's thrash **Big Mind Kill**!"

154

We were shaking just saying her name. "I've been **D**i**squalified** from my fencing competition, right? SO, let's win this one."

I saw Big Mind Kill from afar and I wanted to talk to her before the competition started.

"Ready? Will the force be with you?" I asked, sarcastically.

"The force is what gives a jedi his power. It's an energy field created by all living things. It surrounds us and penetrates us. It binds the galaxy together..." she replied.

She was stunning. A gorgeous girl. And a nerd, just like me.

"YOU'VE JUST QUOTED OBI-WAN KENOBI! GREAT!" I was thrilled!

"You got the quote?! Well, **you are**

great!" she said, and then smiled, looking so much prettier than **Ariana Grande**. The competition was about to start. Big Mind Kill's magnetic field turned George and Nicholas silent. I **WASN'T FEELING ANYTHING SUSPICIOUS.** She was trying to block me, but didn't succeed. **WE LOOKED STRAIGHT INTO EACH OTHER'S EYES...** but I felt a different kind of magnetism between the two of us. She was amazing. Professor Zemeckis gave us **60 seconds** to hand in our answers.

YOU CANNOT USE THE TIME MACHINE FOR YOUR OWN GOALS! YOU COULD CREATE A SPACE-TIME PARADOX!

It was all **very funny** because I wasn't really thinking about solving the Law of Cosines, but rather about Han Solo's quote: "**WONDERFUL GIRL. EITHER I'M GONNA KILL HER OR I'M BEGINNING TO LIKE HER!**"

I didn't know whether to beat her or fall in love with her... I waited for Zemeckis's countdown and when he got to 3, I wrote the answer and gave him my sheet, just like she did. Big Mind Kill and I were **completely synchronized.**

The Math competition had two winners: The Killer Minds and The Ping Pong Theory! Both teams gave the right answers and we tied! I went to Big Mind Kill and grabbed her hand. **SHE SMILED. I was very happy. We were all very happy.** George, Nicholas, Ellen, Big Mind Kill, **THE NEWEST MEMBER OF OUR TEAM**, and I!

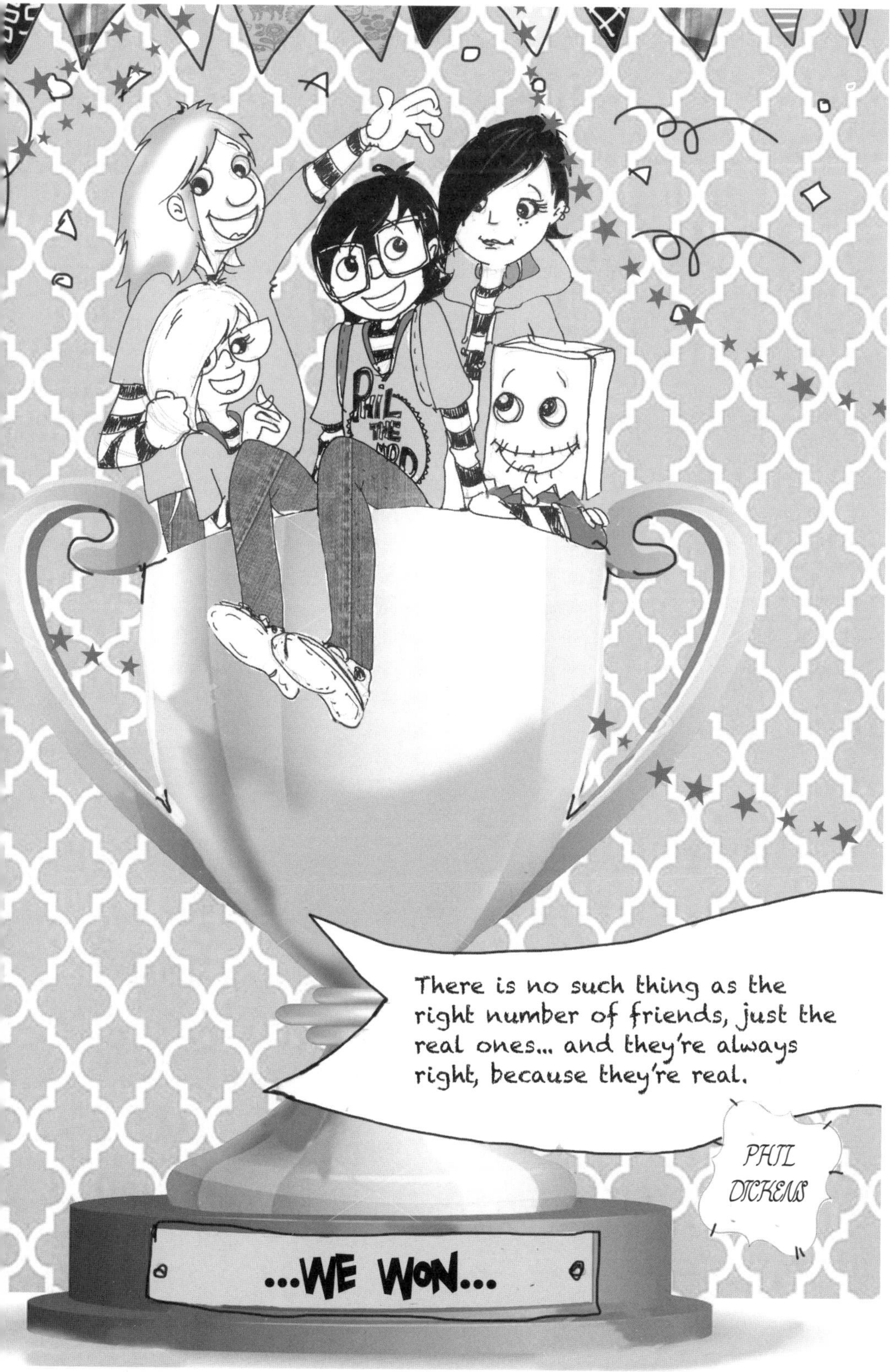
PHIL THE [illegible]
There is no such thing as the right number of friends, just the real ones... and they're always right, because they're real.
PHIL DICKENS
...WE WON...

PHILIP OSBOURNE
DIARY OF A NERD

The story of a very special kid who
believes in fantasy (a lot!)

I'M A
NERD

ACTION

THE THOUSAND
LIGHTS OF
HOLLYWOOD

COMING SOON...
VOLUME TWO!

Buy
the new
graphic
novel

DIRECTOR